Outbound

Gil Hardwick

Published by Crusader eBooks, Perth, Western Australia

Typesetting, Layout and Cover Design by Gil Hardwick

This edition printed and bound by CreateSpace,
https://www.createspace.com/

National Library of Australia Cataloguing-in-Publication entry:

Author: Hardwick, Gil.

Title: Outbound / Gil Hardwick.

ISBN-10: 0-9872987-1-2, ISBN-13: 978-0-9872987-1-3 (paperback)

Dewey Number: A823.4

For Alex,

with special thanks to

Sally-Anne and Patrick

CHAPTERS

Chapter One

The night had been sweltering hot and the great moon low overhead kept the place so bright it was impossible to sleep. It would be full in a day or two and Sam resigned himself to getting a few early jobs completed before the mid-morning sun brought the desert alive with its deceptive citrus greens set against towering outcrops, its shimmering red sand and rolling dunes whiskered by the eternal silver spinifex, stopping them all scorched in their tracks.

The pump was quiet. That was another blessing. The constant whirring hum of the motor and thumping pistons once the sun hit the panels grated on his nerves as if the water did not belong up here on the surface, and lodged its protest at being disturbed so. The aquifer itself was not deep, less than fifty metres, but the ancient liquid had been down there for probably millions of years. It had a right to moan, he had thought early in the piece, and compensated himself by coming down here every morning just as the stars dimmed and all was quiet, as the sky turned instead to face the dawn.

They had a few hours from the time the rising sun hit the panels and the flow of water into the huge network of irrigation pipes began for the day, to when its fury began to be felt and they had to retreat back into the shade. Until then, this was his precious moment to himself in the soft early light.

Making his way across the warm sand small families of colourful finches flew in formation with him, less than a metre from his fingertips as if seeking his intimacy and comfort, and reassurance from him or acknowledgment perhaps. Then they drank their fill for the day before flitting back into the bare acacia branches to make way for the next in turn, where their rainbow breast feathers lit up as the sun broached the horizon, turning the muted pastel shades of the dawn into a fairyland. It cheered him immensely to see them.

Once the sun was up lizards would be out, and black kites would soar overhead looking for trouble and with it a meal or two. Between now and then great flocks of speckled grey-brown pigeons will have come and gone, in serried ranks like the finches, except that the native boys will have had their traps and nets out to snare themselves a good meal ahead of the kites, and the reptiles which they would catch too and eat given half a chance.

This place over the millennia had bred opportunists and they were good at it, given the starkness of contrast between having and having not, which meant going to red dust like the trees and small bushes, and everything else hereabouts aside from the unceasing spinifex. He wondered sometimes whether the people here would thank him for the changes he wrought, before their effect was felt and their way of life altered forever.

Trying to create gardens way out here, now they had permanent water, he sometimes thought a fool's errand. But then, making a shady canopy of fodder trees to bring goats and wild donkeys in close made a lot of sense, and let it evolve from there. Maybe the camels would come in as well. They could always grow melons as ground cover, and yams and other basics, and maybe date palms and citrus. The kangaroos and birds had already come, sensing the water from so far off, and with them their guano to enrich the spent sand.

There was still quite a bit of irrigation to finish, and tree planting back along where the pipes ran to catch any drips and leaks under the low tangled scrub. Early in the piece they decided not to clear the area at all, but to plant under the existing trees and bushes to act as nursery shade for the tender young shoots. The next job would be to protect the gardens from the goats. When they came. They would come. The kites were here already, 200 kilometres south of their natural range, following the flocks of birds which had smelt the water, as the goats would smell it whenever the breeze quartered their way and gradually make their way toward it. It may take another two years; two more winter seasons when the going was easier and they had a chance to survive the crossing over from the coast, but they would come. Eventually they would come.

Too late to worry now, the thing was done. He shrugged and stepped up onto the tank to strip off his hat and boots first, then his shirt and trousers. Stepping tenderly into the crystal clear water under the awning he made his obeisance, then his ablutions, then luxuriated in the cold clear pond waiting for the boys to come running down to take their turn to swim and bathe, and force him out with their noise and splashing about.

Last to use the tank each day were the young warriors who came in at sunset, after a day broken only by their long mid-day siesta. The old men came in of a morning, right after the boys once they had bathed and had their breakfast, and together the two groups would start the day. It was an interesting notion they had adopted, these people, making grandparents and grandchildren brother and sister, and parents the odd ones out. The women would not be here for another week. After their swim in the tank the boys would retreat into the big cavern back up in the breakaway to cook their meal, then spend the whole day with their quiet listening.

He stepped up out of the tank and the grizzled old-timers with their head bands and elaborate scarring from a life of ritual and ceremony nodded to him in passing, while he stepped tenderly around the piles of dead birds and big fat lizards there on the sandy slope. The desert air dried his skin and the effect was so pleasant he delayed dressing until some of the younger men came up with a kangaroo.

They were all watching him. He had lapsed into his dream state and he blinked and shook his head as he came out of it. He pulled on his trousers and boots, then straightening up donned his shirt and hat and went down to meet them. Quietly he led the way down through the older part of the garden through the young orchard trees already making their way up through the scrubby undergrowth. Over to their right they had left a big bare patch where the runoff from the cliff face had carved out a series of dry sandy streamlets, which they had sown instead with deep-rooted clumping buffel grass to stabilise the soil and provide extra fodder. Every time it rained he knew the seeds would sprout further and further downstream until it was too dry altogether and the grass would taper off finally into the desert proper, where the spinifex would take over once more. Already the kangaroos were in there at night, and if all went well they thought to bring in a few head of cattle.

As the sun rose and the pump started they were making their way through a new patch of desert acacias when one of the men stopped suddenly. It was quiet and shady under the low canopy so they all paused and watched for his sign. Nothing doing, one by one they followed his gaze to see a battered Landcruiser topping the distant crest of a dune in their direction, headlights on high beam and engine revving as the faint sound came to them on the still morning air. They stood and watched as it disappeared, then after a while reappeared atop the next red dune, then for the next half hour while it slowly came closer and closer. One of the men muttered something in his own language, and Sam turned to ask what was said.

"He say, nobody driving, boss."

Sam looked out over the desert as the truck drew closer and closer. They could see clean through the cab, yet it followed the track well enough.

His brow furrowed slightly but he said nothing.

Eventually the vehicle came in along the track approaching the gardens where they were standing under the shade, and he stepped out into the sandy wheel ruts and waited for it to come up alongside. It kept coming and coming at him and at the very last moment he jumped aside to let it pass. As it did so he looked down through the open driver's side window to see a dirty tousle-haired boy at the wheel staring up at him in astonishment, so he mounted the running board and reaching his hand through the window turned off the ignition. The truck ground suddenly to a stop and he stepped down and opened the door.

The boy fell out into his arms. He was filthy and obviously exhausted from lack of sleep, and all he could murmur was, "Snake. Snake got him. Big snake . . . . "

By then the men were crowding around, and soon a soft voice from the back of the truck caused him to put the boy down and go see what was happening. A tall man lay stretched out on the floor under the canopy with his bare feet hanging over the swinging tailgate. He was obviously quite dead; somewhat bloated and discoloured, so after a brief parley he sent one of the men up to get one of his still cameras and record the scene. That done he picked up the boy while someone started the truck and drove back along the track some distance where they stopped. One of them took a shovel from the back and began digging a grave.

Sam carried the boy up through the gardens and over to the tank where he set him down again and stripped off his filthy rags. He then stripped his own clothes again and picking him up carried him into the water. The boy shuddered slightly at the sudden cold but he sucked and licked thirstily at the wet hand lifted to his mouth and washing his face, then relaxed and allowed himself to be bathed and cleaned. He had been badly dehydrated and having him drink too much water would sicken and weaken him, so keeping him there to soak helped replenish body fluids directly through his skin as he lay there in his lap for another half-hour or so, cool water splashing onto his head and face.

As he carried him out of the pool finally and stood him up on the rock shelf to dry with his shirt, it occurred to him that he might be a good bit older than he had first appeared. He was short but had a good layer of puppy fat indicating growth ahead; twelve at least by the look of him.

He stood him there while he dried himself off and pulled on his own trousers. As he did so it struck him oddly that the filthy rags neither fit the picture somehow. Bending slightly he turned the boy around and checked him over. Aside from signs of a long journey he bore no old scaring from scraped knees and shins, and elbows and forearms, that might be expected of a street kid or any of these rough native boys knocking themselves about endlessly. He neither had their lean hard torso and trim, well-defined muscle tone, or rough hands and splayed feet. His face was gaunt and eyes hollow from exhaustion, his hands chapped with blisters, and his nails were dirty and broken, but he was nonetheless a handsome boy in the classic style; well proportioned, and would grow into a fine looking adult. When he opened his mouth to check he saw that all his teeth were sound and straight, only needing a clean with a good toothbrush to bring them back into order.

Satisfied that he was basically healthy Sam picked him up bodily and carried him up into the main cave where the boys and old men gathered around curiously. One of the older boys came over with a pair of shorts and he slipped them on his now shivering charge, then made way as he picked him up again and carried him over to the small side cave where he slept slightly away from the main group. There he put him down gently on his swag.

The boy who had loaned his spare shorts came over with some roasted pigeon and yams, and breaking small pieces off and chewing them into a pulp began feeding his new charge, making sure that he chewed and swallowed each morsel before taking the next wad from his mouth and pressing it gently to his lips. Before long he took the whole bird on his own account and started nibbling at it himself, causing the other to nod and smile brightly. He gave him some roast potato then and he took that too and ate it, but when he was offered more he declined and lay down on the swag.

"What is your name, boy?" Sam wanted to know.

"Obi-wan Kenobi."

"Is that it? Do you have a surname, or a family to belong?"

"I don't know," he shrugged and shook his head.

"All right. My name is Sam. Sam Flanagan. This boy is Peter. His full name is Peter Wilson Napantjarra. I call him little brother. You call him brother as well, all right."

The boy nodded, then, "Where is George? Is he alive?"

"Is that his name? George who?"

"George Summers. His name is George Summers. He told me. Is he all right?"

"He is dead. He has been dead for a day or so. We had to bury him straight away. The men are doing that now."

He looked from face to face then nodded again, quietly to himself.

"Cranky old bastard. Good riddance anyway. I told him not to poke that snake. It came right at him, and into him. Kept biting him." He looked up again and shook his head as if to rid himself of a dread memory, then lay down and rolling over to face the wall pulled the rough blanket up over his shoulders, and lay there awhile not saying anything.

Sam touched Peter lightly on the arm and together they stood and slipped quietly out into the cave proper where everyone had crowded around waiting patiently. The mood was sombre; all these bearded old men with their patterned ceremonial scarring and red head-bands, with wide-eyed boys gathered reverently about them; the roof blackened by millennia of camp fires, and all along the back wall ancestral figures in all shades of red, yellow and white ochre and charcoal black parading in ethereal splendour.

There was nothing much to be said so he simply shrugged and walked outside, while they all turned away and went back to their business. Over at the tank he donned his remaining clothes, and dressed again made his way back down through the gardens to where the men were working steadily now at their set tasks.

Chapter Two

Sam was annoyed and distracted. This sort of thing had happened to him far too often and he was increasingly suspicious that something was up. Perhaps the boy was a messenger from somebody, maybe not. What was a boy like him doing way out here? Holding him in his arms as he did he felt no disturbance, so he was sure he was guilty of nothing in himself, but who had sent him?

Ignoring the men in the garden for the moment he walked out along the track to where the truck was parked under the spare she-oak standing out there by itself. The grave itself was in order. They had gathered a pile of flat rocks and arranged them neatly over the disturbed area to stop the dingoes digging it up, so he paced back and forth with his GPS handset getting a fix on the site before sitting down in the shade to record the event in his field diary.

Turning his attention to the truck he went over it, searching under the seats and every nook and cranny before emptying the glove box and a bag of tools out onto a square of canvas on the ground; then everything from the tucker box, cooking utensils, everything he could find. There was another box full of prospecting gear and he emptied that too. Then he took down a rifle and a shotgun from their mounting behind the seat and stripped them, then emptied all of the ammunition onto the canvas as well.

He picked through it all carefully but there was nothing there save what anyone around the bush would ordinarily carry, so he packed everything neatly and put it all back just as he had found it.

The vehicle itself was in good enough order, and both firearms were clean and kept well oiled. All water and fuel tanks were well supplied. The man must have been a fair mechanic since there were no dodgy farmyard repairs evident either, beyond the fact that some of the gear was starting to show its age which was natural. The loud engine revving he realised had been brought on by the boy driving all that way in first gear, not being properly able to reach the clutch and work the brakes at the same time.

To check all was well he got in and started the engine, then drove back to the garden where he parked under some good shade and got out again. The men had a small fire going there and were roasting another kangaroo. What he wanted to know was whether they had found anything on the body; anything at all unusual or unexpected. They glanced at one another and shook their heads. There was nothing. It was starting to smell quite badly and the bowel had opened as they picked it up off the truck, making them hurry, but if there was anything else they would have noticed.

Leaving the truck where it was under the leafy canopy he walked back up through the gardens toward the big cavern. Passing the tank he distracted himself for a moment to pick through the boy's rags. He had obviously not bathed for some time, or washed his clothes at any rate. Apart from the rank, musty smell the pockets were empty. There was nothing else either; nothing stitched into any seam, nothing embroidered; nothing. They might have been picked up from an opportunity shop or somebody's charity bin, then worn threadbare. But this boy was no urchin. This boy had an air about him. He was plainly intelligent and well spoken. There was something else but he could not quite put his finger on it. Not yet.

The brightening day was starting seriously to heat up. Tired from so little sleep the night before, and somewhat perturbed now at this intrusion, he wandered up the slope to the great overhanging cavern and went in. In the side chamber Peter was sitting guard patiently over the sleeping boy while several of the old men looked up at him as he glanced about. Rather than acknowledge them he simply sighed and shrugged, then without ado took some spare blankets from his gear and spread them on the soft sand. He caught Peter's eye and nodded slightly, then stripping off his shirt and boots lay down on the blankets and forced himself to sleep. He was not hungry and anyway there would be food for him when he woke, so after a moment of contemplation he shut down his mind and drifted off.

It was scorching hot outside when he did wake finally. It must be just after noon by the feel of it. The boy was already sitting up picking delicately at a big fat goanna, eating slowly and steadily one piece at a time, so Sam lay there collecting his thoughts. After a while he noticed the other watching him, then on his nod pass some of the meat across on a bed of fresh leaves. After he had eaten a little he sat picking at the carcass as well before looking up directly. The boy calling himself Obi was staring at him intently, eyes wide and face open, not from fear but a degree of recognition.

"Do you know me from somewhere?" he asked gently, but the boy continued staring at him curiously awhile then shrugged and slowly shook his head.

"Are you feeling all right now?" he persisted.

"Yes. Just tired."

Peter murmured to him softly, then called gently to someone in the main cavern, and he nodded before turning back to the boy.

"Do you know where you are?"

"No, not really . . . in the desert somewhere."

"Is that so? Where did you meet George?"

"I don't remember. I was a bit lost. It was dark and I had nowhere to sleep, so he let me sleep in the truck. Then he said he had to go see someone out in the desert, and would I like to come along for the ride. This morning I had a thought maybe someone was you. I don't know, I've seen you somewhere before."

"Why would he want to see me?"

The other shrugged and shook his head.

At the point Peter stood and went across to the entrance, then came back slowly with a thin, gnarled, shriveled old man at his arm, carefully making his way with the aid of a big black old stick quite as gnarled as he was, as if it were part of himself. He was obviously blind, but treated with great reverence and respect. Even Sam stood as he approached, and together they sat him down next to the swag where the boy sat. He laid his stick on the sand between them then sat quietly waiting.

"You must call this man grandfather, son. He is a doctor, and he will examine you. Is that all right with you?"

Obi recoiled slightly, but nodded. They watched him intently as the old man gazed steadily at him through sightless eyes, then he began to shiver though it was still quite hot here inside the cave. Presently he broke out in goose bumps, and started to sweat, and as they watched they could see his boyhood tumescence standing up, tenting the fabric of his borrowed shorts. Peter said something softly to his grandfather who stopped, and Obi visibly relaxed.

"What's happening, boy?" Sam wanted to know.

"He is invading me. He wants to know my secrets."

"Do you have secrets?"

The boy stared wide-eyed, and shivered, then drew back into himself tucking his knees up close to his chest and wrapped his arms protectively around them. The old man sat waiting again.

Peter shook his head then leaning over to Sam said quietly, "Something the matter, boss."

"Obi, do you know what this place is?"

He shook his head.

"This place is called Puntayeri. It's a bush camp, bush holiday camp. Two road business. That means, we bring the boys out here during school holidays to learn traditional law, and learn country. This is a big ritual centre for these people. They live at Warmunya where the kids go to school, but this place is very important to them. That's why Vincent is here. He is the chief law man right across, proper big law man. He does not mean you harm, but he will know everything about you. You cannot hide anything from him."

"Vincent? Is this Vincent? This old bloke?" Obi was no longer listening but sat looking steadily at the ancient wizened skeleton of an old man seated patiently before him.

"Do you know him? Do you know who he is?"

He gazed back and forth between the two, then looked away to sit silently staring at the wall of the cave. He stopped shivering, and Sam leaned forward again to catch his attention. Nothing doing he put his hand out and touched him on the knee causing him to start suddenly.

"We need to get this done. If it is uncomfortable for you just lie down and Vincent will put you to sleep until he is finished. Nobody will harm you. Peter and I will wait outside with the others."

"No. Don't go."

They continued to watch him closely.

"He is going to die as well. Vincent is going to die too."

The old man giggled at that, softly, knowingly, to himself. "Too right," he chuckled. "Close up pinish now, tis pella."

Peter started chuckling as well. "That not your fault, brother," he said merrily. "This 'is last trip now, this grandfather, then 'e finish up properly. Become country now, properly, this old man. Pretty soon. Everybody happy. No worry."

The boy looked as if he were going to protest further when Vincent flicked his fingers suddenly and he collapsed sideways onto the swag like a rag doll. They laid him out straight on his back, and the old man promptly started singing over him. The song went on and on, and as he sang he passed his hands back and forth along the young body, until eventually he stopped as abruptly as he started and indicated for Peter to take his hand and help him up. They left the boy asleep there on the swag, just as he was without trying to cover him in any way since it was still very hot, and moved across to a far corner of the cavern where they settled again.

Vincent began singing once more, this time at a slow, measured pace allowing Peter to keep up with him while he translated, pausing occasionally where he misheard or struggled over some of the words. Sam knew well enough not to interrupt the flow, so he sat quietly with eyes half closed listening to the steady rhythmic chant with one ear, and absorbing the flow of information from Peter with the other.

When they were finished he went back across to the swag and woke Obi, who simply yawned and stretched, then looking at him blankly for a moment turned over and went back to sleep. Nothing doing, he turned and went across to his spare blankets and rolled himself up in them, and slept himself. Peter led his grandfather out and handed him over to the old men in the main cavern, then came back and sat quietly to keep his vigil.

Chapter Three

During the night Sam lit a small kerosene pressure lamp by which to write. Peter brought some spare blankets in from the main cavern and set Obi there to sleep beside him, allowing Sam to have his swag back. As he sat updating his journal they both watched him intently as boys do, murmuring softly to one another and only occasionally interrupting him to explain this or that. Eventually he stopped writing and looked across at them sitting there together, his brow furrowing with curiosity.

He cocked his head, one to the other, then finally, "Can you write, son?" he asked Obi.

"Of course I can. I'll show you."

He marked his page then opened the back cover and passed the journal across, and handed him his pen. The boy took the book and placed it across his knees, and taking the pen in his right hand thought a moment then wrote a few lines and passed it back.

Sam looked. It was a poem he had remembered from school, long ago, rendered in a boy's hand more than slightly extrovert and oversize. It read:

> Abou Ben Adhem (may his tribe increase!)
> Awoke one night from a deep dream of peace,
> And saw, within the moonlight in his room,
> Making it rich, and like a lily in bloom,
> An Angel writing in a book of gold:

He glanced up at him, thoughtfully. "Can you give me the rest of it?" he asked.

Obi nodded and took a deep breath, then in his broken treble recited the whole poem, word-perfect.

"Bravo!" Sam exclaimed while the other sat grinning from ear to ear, and Peter simply looked on astonished. "Where did you learn that?"

"I don't know. I just know it."

"Is that so? What else do you know?"

"Quite a lot. I was dux at school. Or nearly. I would have been."

"All right. Do you know how old you are, or when is your birthday?"

"Nothing. I don't know anything like that. I don't remember."

"But you knew how to write, and you remembered that poem. Who wrote it?"

"James Henry Leigh Hunt, 1784 to 1859. But that's school work. We have to remember that . . . for exams . . . . ," he started to reply but stumbled, then looked at them and shivered, and drew back into himself.

Sam glanced at Peter briefly and he stood and left, returning shortly with Vincent hobbling along holding onto his arm, and his big old stick out in front.

Obi withdraw a little further into himself, until Sam glanced across and asked, "Where did you get the name 'Obi-wan'? You remembered that all right?"

"Obi-wan Kenobi. Star Wars. That's my nick-name from school. I am Jedi."

"Something happened to you, is that right?"

Obi stared at him a moment and nodded slightly, then gazed away into the distance.

"Vincent is going to sit with us now, is that all right? Does that worry you?"

He shook his head slightly without moving.

"He is going to hypnotise you again, just a little. He is not going to knock you out like he did today. He knows everything about you now so he doesn't need to worry. You don't need to worry. This time it will only be shallow, enough to break through whatever is stopping you from remembering for yourself, so we can ask you some questions."

Obi nodded again, loosening a little, and his eyes coming back into focus he stood and went across to help Peter with Vincent who set his stick aside and took his hand instead. Sam took a folded blanket and together they sat the old man down on it, then Obi went back and brought his stick and set it in front of him. Old Vincent found and held his shoulder while he groped for his stick there on the sand, and having located it drew it close. Letting go of him he leaned back against the rock face.

Sam waited awhile then looked up at Obi and across to Peter, who simply shrugged.

"Who is Auntie Edie, Obi?"

"Nanna's sister. She looked after me when Nanna died."

"Who is Nanna?"

"My grandmother, Dad's mother."

"Who is your father?"

"He is a boss."

"How big a boss?"

"Very big boss."

"What happened to your mother?"

Obi paused a moment. "She died when I was little."

"Are you all right about that?"

"Yes." He glanced away, then back again. "It wasn't her fault. She had cancer."

"What happened then?"

"Well, I don't know, things just sort of happened."

"Your Nanna died too, a bit later."

"Yes."

"So who is Ysabella?"

Obi's face snapped open and he stared, eyes wide, then bunched himself up again and started to shiver. His hand crept down to his groin as if to cover himself, despite the fact that he was still wearing shorts, then absently started to stroke himself with his thumb through the course fabric, gazing off into the far distance.

"Dad's new girlfriend," he turned and said finally. Then he reddened, and giggled slightly, and shook his head again as if ridding himself of another bad thought, but finally he turned and blurted out, "He went ballistic when he found out. She told him it was me, that it was my fault, that I was a randy little shit, but it wasn't me it was her all the time. She wouldn't leave me alone."

"Told him what?"

"What?"

"Told him what, Obi?"

"He came home early one night when she was fucking with me in his bed, sucking my dick. She was always fooling around like that and wouldn't leave me alone, even sometimes when he was home, downstairs in his study. Even when I was having a shower she would get in with me. Then he found out. That's what happened."

"What does your father do?"

"He is a media big stick, and property developer. Real big bickies."

He did not say any more after that, just leaned back against the rock facing staring back into the distance and let the tears run. Eventually they let him go, and not long after that he simply lay down on his blankets and went to sleep. Peter helped Vincent up and took him back to his own sleeping place in the main cavern, then came back and lay down beside Obi on his blankets and went off to sleep as well. Sam sat up finishing the final design layout for the last of the garden. Satisfied with it he leaned across and shut the pressure lamp fuel valve, and when it sputtered out rolled over onto his swag and lay awhile thinking.

Just on daylight next morning as the big camp began to stir he got up and went to have a quick parley with Vincent and the group of elders. They murmured quietly among themselves, then simply nodded and settled back on their blankets. Returning to the side cavern he gently woke the two sleeping boys and spoke briefly with them. Peter was no longer to sit with the younger boys, but both were to join the men's work detail in the gardens. In future they would both sleep in here with him because it was too hot anyway under the bough shelters outside, but apart from that not a word was to be said to anyone about what had happened to Obi.

Peter already knew what the penalty was, for that sort of thing, and that was to be the end of it as far as the camp was concerned. He was just another of the boys coming of age, here by circumstance. They would sort the rest out as they went along.

Sam motioned them both up and they went outside quietly ahead of the main rush. There were a few of the older boys out already, returning from setting their nets and traps around the edge of the garden. Just past the truck Obi stopped and turned back to look at it, then back again to Sam.

"George is dead, right? I mean, he died, didn't he?"

"Yes, he is dead. They buried him under that old she-oak, that one over there by itself." He turned to point to the tree a hundred metres or so away, and the fresh mound nearby.

Obi looked about, then stepped quickly around to the back of the truck and kneeling down reached his arm right in under the tailgate. He fumbled around for a moment then withdrew his hand and stood smiling, holding a dirty cotton ore bag containing something heavy. He had to carry it in both hands. He walked over to Sam and gave it to him.

"It's mine just as much as it was his. I did all the work. Not the sapphires, or the opals, I don't mean them," he leaned in close and spoke softly. "I didn't dig them, he had them with him when he came over from Queensland, but the gold is mine. I dug it all out by myself."

Then he looked up and shook his head. "It doesn't make any difference now, does it? I mean, it's all mine, isn't it? George is dead."

Sam looked around quickly, then half turning put the bag into his satchel next to his diary and maps. He glanced across at Peter one finger to his lips, and the other simply cocked his head slightly. Without further ado they made their way down into the garden proper where the men were just stirring under their bough shelters.

One of the older men came up behind them as they approached, back from relieving himself, and said quietly, "What's up, boss?"

They turned, and Sam introduced him to Obi. "This man is Bertram. You call him father, all right? He will be your boss during the day."

Then he repeated briefly his earlier discussion with the senior elders up in the cavern and the other nodded.

The exchange completed he turned to both boys. "You eat here now as well. This is your fire now, here with these men. If the other boys give you anything, any birds or anything else they catch, you must bring it and cook it here. When you finish your work every day you will go to the tank with these men. You are not to bathe any more with the young boys.

When you have done that come up to the cave and sleep there with me. Is that clear?"

They both nodded and he turned on his heel and started back up the slope. After he had gone a few paces he stopped again and indicated for Obi to follow him a little way. Just out of earshot he stopped and standing in close asked him quietly, "What was she like, son?"

The boy looked up sharply, mouth agape. "A real doll," he said. "She is gorgeous. I don't know where he finds them."

Then he stopped, and shrugged, shaking his head. He looked into Sam's face and added, "After my mother died Dad sort of went all strange, and started playing up a lot and having all these big flash parties with all these beautiful people. I don't know, I think he just forget I was there."

"All right, thank you for that." He turned to go, then stopped again patting his satchel, but as the boy nodded he went on his way, back up into the cave from where he re-emerged presently and went down to the tank for his morning swim.

Chapter Four

Another week went by and they settled into their routine. Occasionally a fresh afternoon breeze sprang up from far to the west but other than that it was just plain debilitating hot. The men worked every day from just before dawn until mid-morning; as soon as there was enough light to see by, then stopped and played cards or dozed or talked quietly together until late afternoon when the heat abated and they could start work again. Both boys were tired of an evening now. When they came up from their swim and changed into fresh clothes for the night they would both drop off straight to sleep.

The day the women were due to arrive came and went. Next day some of the men waited up along the track to keep an eye out for them, calling back and forth to each other the whole afternoon while the camp became increasingly unsettled. Early in the evening Bertram came over and politely suggested that at dawn next morning they take two of the trucks and go look for them. One of their vehicles might have broken down, or they may have simply been late starting out anyway. Nobody knew what was happening since they could not raise them on the two-way radio either, so early evening they busied themselves refueling two of the newer Landcruisers and topping up the water tanks.

During the night Sam lay dozing. He had done his journal and as was his habit lain awake awhile thinking before nodding off. A slight disturbance behind him brought him awake and he half turned to feel Obi settling himself alongside him on the swag. He shifted across to accommodate him, then as he did not move rolled over again and began drifting back to sleep.

"Sam," the boy said finally, and when he didn't answer nudged him with his elbow.

"Yes. What is it, son?"

"What's happening?"

"They are worried the women and babies might be stuck out there in the desert. They were supposed to have been here yesterday and somebody needs to go see what has happened."

"Will they be all right?"

"Yeah, for a day or two. The main thing is if they run out of water. It can be a close call this far out."

"We can take George's truck."

"What makes you think you are going?"

"I know where they might be. I think they're back up there where the snake got George. We got bogged there and like, George did his nut. He lost his temper and cut the track up real bad trying to get out. Then when he finally got the truck out there was this big snake there and he went after it with a stick. That's when it turned around and came at him."

"Is that right?"

"Yes. If another truck came through there they would have to go around, or they'd go in right up to the axles."

Sam pondered that a moment, then sat up reaching for his little pressure lamp.

"Didn't you pull some logs or branches across to warn people, or leave a mark they could read, anything like that?" he asked, almost aside.

Obi stared at him helplessly in the dark. "I didn't know. I'm just a kid, Sam. I was trying to help George. I don't know, everything just went haywire suddenly."

"All right, it's not your fault. Come with me, eh, we had better let everyone know."

Sam lit the lamp and standing with it led the way outside. There was a huge gibbous moon still up and plenty of light so they went straight down the path into the gardens, Sam calling softly ahead so as not to come onto the sleeping men suddenly out of the shadows. The camp stirred at their approach, then Bertram called back his reply and they stopped there to wait for him.

Sam explained the situation briefly, then they both probed Obi for information on how far back up the track they might be, and what other landmarks might help to pinpoint the location. At length Bertram flicked his head up in recognition, and turning quickly on his heel went back and spoke brusquely to some of the men.

As they went to start the trucks Obi stepped forward as if to go with them but Sam grabbed him by the shoulder and held him back.

"Where do you think you're going, young fellow?" he wanted to know.

"I can show them where to go," he replied.

Sam chuckled and shook his head. "These men are warriors and this is their traditional country. You're only a boy, and you have no place here anyway. No, this is serious business, you'll only annoy them getting in the way like that."

"But can't we lend them George's truck, and save them their petrol and water? It's a lot better equipped than theirs."

"Ah, you have a lot to learn, don't you? No. Leave it be. They like you, don't worry about that, but you haven't yet earned your place among them. You haven't even earned your place among the children, you need to understand that."

"Ha!" Obi mocked suddenly, angry at the insult, and pushed him away. "My father is Jack Lennox! I'm not some child, you can't fool me."

"What? Lennox? Jack Lennox? The Lennox boy? Is that you?" Sam gazed at him intently, nodding slowly in recognition. "Alexander Lennox, is it? I'll be damned. The whole bloody country is out looking for you."

Obi started to protest but Sam caught him by the shoulder and shoved him ahead back up to the cave, shaking his head as he did so. Back inside he lay down on his swag and motioned the boy to go back to sleep as well, it was too early in the morning and he was tired.

Mid-morning as they were packing up ready to retire from the sweltering sun the convoy of vehicles arrived, led by Bertram in his Landcruiser followed by a great big tray-back safari truck with drop down sides covered by a loose canvas canopy. Two more trucks drove up behind, then finally taking up the rear came the second of their own camp vehicles. The front and back vehicles had heavy chains draped around their front bull bars, and hi-lift jacks out for ready use.

Everyone was plainly weary and glad to be here, so while the camp poured out to welcome them Sam took Obi by the arm and held him back awhile to sit under a tree with him and watch. The crowd eventually began to organise itself with different families spreading out and setting up small camps of their own, scattered around the garden in various directions, and soon the younger boys took their bits of gear down from the big cave where they had stayed with the old men, and went down to join their parents. Late in the day several trucks drove out again, hunting further afield now to cater for the extra mouths to feed, and as the days went by a tangible shift in the routine made itself felt.

Up in the main cavern the old men stayed to enjoy the peace and quiet as several of their old wives came up to join them there. A steady stream of visitors came to sit with Vincent and their quiet conversations droned on and on. Sam abandoned work in the garden and sat with them to take notes as they recited their stories. Occasionally they would call Obi in too, to look at him and have him repeat his story to them over and over until eventually he too made it his habit to sit there, and watch and listen.

The next night he was lying on his blankets, half awake watching Sam busy again with his journal, and he got up to sit close beside him on the swag.

"What is it, son?" the other wanted to know, glancing thoughtfully at him between lines.

"Why are you always writing? You never stop."

"This is my field diary. I'm preparing my doctoral thesis on these people."

"What in?"

"Anthropology. Landscape ethnography: Aboriginal history; land rights, traditional society and culture, land ownership. That is what I do."

"Really? You some sort of academic?"

"Yes. I have to complete my two years field work first, then when I go back I have another two or three years to write it up. I have a sort of deal going with these people. I help them with their various projects and they tell me their stories, and about themselves." Then he turned and looked squarely at him. "Right now, to be honest, I am thinking of a chapter about you arriving."

"Me? What about?"

"Not much, just the way you arrived and how they responded. Old Vincent says there is a legend here about a mad boy who becomes one of the people, so they are making a big dance about it. There is a big dance coming up in a day or two."

Obi sat quietly for a few moments, then asked softly, "It won't get me into trouble, will it?"

"Why would it get you into trouble?" Then he turned back to his writing and went on awhile before continuing. "Is there something else you need to be telling us?"

"You already know."

"Know what? There are some things we think we know but there are whole parts of the story that don't make any sense at all, apart from what Peter has translated from Vincent. We still need you to fill in a few more gaps."

"What gaps?"

"I'm not sure yet. Something to do with the police and somebody else, and there was a big building, and you climbed out a window. Then there was a train, and you changed your clothes for some reason. What was that all about?"

"It wasn't fair. It's not fair, Sam."

"What wasn't fair?"

"Dad went off his brain at me for fucking with Ysabella. I told you that. I went to stay over at my mate's place, and I told him what happened. We were talking about it next day at school and one of the teachers heard us so she reported it. The headmaster threw a real wobbly. Then the shit hit the fan with police and child welfare all over the place, asking me all these stupid questions, so I ran away. I caught the train from Melbourne all the way up to Cairns. I thought I might cut across to Darwin. When I got to Cairns I changed my clothes at the Op Shop bin and starting hitching. But I had to come back down through Camooweal, and just after that George picked me up. Instead of going on up to Darwin he brought me across here and made me work for him."

"All right, that makes sense. So, what are you planning to do next? You can't keep running forever."

"Yes I know. I've been thinking about that. Can I stay here with you?"

"I won't be here much longer," Sam looked at him, "Not this trip anyway. I have to go south and report to my supervisor. Then I was going to take a break for a month or so, and come back here after the Wet Season. Next trip I am taking Peter back down with me to start school. He is enrolled at the university college on a scholarship. But we still need to get you sorted out, don't we?"

The boy nodded while Sam sucked his pen, nervously twirling it in his fingers thinking to himself awhile before nodding. "All right. You can come with me to Adelaide when I leave, assuming everything is in order. Tomorrow we'll radio in to the mission to report Alexander Lennox found safe and well, then we'll take it from there."

"Thanks, Sam," and without saying anything further Obi rolled onto his own blankets and curling up in them went to sleep.

Chapter Five

The new moon came and went, and over the next two weeks tension in the camp began to build. Whole groups disappeared for hours at a time, early in the morning and late afternoon, while at the back of the big cavern people came and sat with the senior elders who sang to them softly and went over and over their story lines and dance steps with them. Every night Sam sat up writing, and Obi got into the habit of sitting with him reading over his shoulder and making comments until finally, exasperated, he took a new journal from his things and gave it to him, with some spare pencils.

He turned out to be a fair artist, and sat day after day from that point making sketches and small portraits of people as they went about their preparations. Looking at his work one evening, Sam took a small field camera and gave it to him, then next evening went through the day's shots with him and satisfied with his efforts gave him the job of still photographer. That led to them both sitting up talking about cameras and light and angles, at which Sam unpacked his big digital television camera as well and showed him how to use it.

They were paying no attention whatever, then, when next day as they were making their way down through the gardens suddenly a group of men painted and decorated with feathers sprang from the undergrowth. Grabbing Obi by both arms they dragged him yelling away into the scrub. As Sam turned to go after him some of the men barred him, rattling their spears and threatening until he backed away and they disappeared after the others.

Away up and over the ridge coming down off the breakaway they raced while he tripped and stumbled in his bare feet. There was a big old clearing through some trees there, and they halted a moment while one of the men behind reached down and pulled off his shorts before continuing with him into the big circle of boys standing there as naked as he, and surrounded likewise by small groups of men. All assembled they were led away, disappearing among the rocks.

The enormous red disc of a moon appeared on the horizon finally, and quickly rose to break off into the sky proper, brightening to a silver-white glow as it did so. Directly opposite the sun dipped and vanished. With only a brief shift in light intensity while the celestial exchange took place and fires were lit, the cleared area rapidly flooded with brightness. At that moment, off to the side a mass stamping and shouting was heard which quickly settled into a steady beating rhythm accompanying by the sharp click of song sticks and boomerangs. Then the deep throaty growl of didgeridoos began, and on cue long lines of dancers appeared.

The women came first, all together, then retreated to form a long backdrop to the scene allowing small groups of women to come out ahead and dance, each after their own form, before retreating again into the backdrop. It was nearly an hour before they finished, then abruptly a hoarse shout came from off-stage and a long line of men came high-stepping prancing across shepherding the boys, who came on dancing likewise.

Each group of boys then stepped out and danced in their turn. Sam watched delightedly as Peter and Obi came up together clad in hair belt and pubic tassel, and with feathers in their hair. Obi was painted with a great snake writhing around the whole length of his torso, surrounded by intricate designs, while from Peter shone what looked like storm and lightning. He set the big camera focused on them and as they came close into the firelight and danced together in perfect unison he let it run.

When they had all finished another group of men came prancing up, chasing them off, while a third group came up behind to form a backdrop as the women had done. Suddenly, amid a loud series of brolga calls Bertram burst onto the stage and took their breath away with the most delicate leaping, swooping, fluttering movements for such a big, heavy-set man. They were spell-bound. The performance was extraordinary. As he disappeared off-stage as suddenly he reappeared again with four other men, while at once the boys came in from stage opposite and joined them in the circle. The clacking sticks and didgeridoos and massed voices rose into a crescendo, and with that abruptly everything stopped and the stage cleared. Everyone seemed to have disappeared and the night went completely quiet.

After a while Sam packed his gear and made his way slowly and thoughtfully back through the gardens then up the slope to the big cave. The whole area was deathly quiet, with only the great bright moon now directly overhead accompanying him to his quarters. Before going inside he turned to gaze out over the now silent plain, only small flashes of movement through the trees below betraying the presence of others, and he shook his head marveling at the way this place drew him back season after season.

Inside he lit his little lamp but instead of writing he sat on his swag with his back against the wall, staring off into the distance. Some time later Obi came in, more or less cleaned up. He had managed to recover his shorts though they now bore a big rip across the backside showing bare cheek through the torn cloth, but without saying anything at all he rolled up in his swag and went off to sleep. Just as he did so Peter entered in much the same condition and did likewise, except that he had lost his shorts and bore a strip of shirt around his hips in obeisance to modesty, but he dropped that as he lay down and promptly curled up in his blankets as well.

At the first glimmer of daylight next morning Sam went out into the main cave and rummaged through stray piles of clothing that had accumulated there over the period, and choosing several pairs of shorts about the right size and a shirt each, he went back and woke the boys. Together they went down to the tank for a decent bath. It was there that he decided on impulse to clear out straight away and he promptly announced his decision. Both boys looked intensely at him, then scrambled out of the tank and still dripping wet slipped on their shorts and shirts and ran off down to the main camp.

By the time he had his gear packed they had returned to help him carry everything to the truck. Last thing, he dug in the sand beneath the place his swag had lain and taking out the cotton ore-sample bag brushed off the dirt and placed it carefully in a spare compartment in his camera case. Clasping it shut he carried it down too and stowed it neatly in front of the driver's seat just under his legs. At the last minute Bertram came strolling over, and quietly suggested that he take George's truck instead. He looked at him for a moment, then nodded thoughtfully.

None of the people there would use it because the dead body had been in the back. They were afraid of the ghost still hanging around until the proper ceremonies could be held sometime next year, or the year after if ever.

So they unpacked everything and carried it across to the other truck and stowed it carefully, then after thinking about it a moment Sam took both firearms from their rack behind the seat and wrapped them in canvas. Signaling the boys to bring the ammunition, up in the small side cavern where they had slept he hid everything high up on a rock shelf, well back out of sight. Returning to the truck he walked around looking it over. Nothing appeared out of the ordinary that would make anyone stop and investigate, apart from the good tools and prospecting gear, and tucker box and things. Satisfied, Sam backed it out from under the trees and drove it across to the fuel tank where he topped up both main and auxiliary tanks. There was plenty of water so he wiped his hands on his trousers and got into the cab where he noticed both boys sitting there in the truck waiting for him.

He leaned past Obi and asked Peter where he was going, but both sat there mute, looking straight ahead through the windscreen.

"You can't come, Peter. Next trip, eh? Right now I have to escort Alex to the police station in Tennant Creek. And we have to report George's death, and hand his truck in. Then we are going on to Adelaide for a week or so. Then we have to go across to Melbourne to sort out this mess with his family. I am not coming back up here again for months," he explained.

The words had no effect.

Sam stepped out of the cab then and went quickly over to where Bertram patiently waited and explained the situation to him as well, but the other waved him on, shaking his head. Peter was going to Adelaide to start school. It was all arranged. He looked at him, startled, then back at the truck, and resigning himself got back in and started the engine ready to go.

At that point Obi stopped his hand and said to wait while he scrambled quickly over Peter. Jumping down onto the track he ran back up into the main cave. Vincent was lying back there on his side with his head propped up on a pillow as one of the old women fed him soup from a bowl, and Obi stood there watching them a moment.

Presently the old man brushed the spoon aside and stared at the boy with his rheumy, sightless old eyes, then abruptly started to cry. Obi stepped across and dropped onto his knees in the sand in front of him, but neither spoke as tears streamed down their cheeks, until one of the women touched him gently on the shoulder and motioned him to go.

He stood at that, then turning away ran straight out without looking behind, and back at the truck climbed up over Peter again and sat there beside Sam, shaking his head occasionally until finally he broke up and threw his head back and wailed out loud. His keening started others off in the garden and among the trees. The shrill sound echoed back and forth, right up onto the breakaway above the caves.

Eventually through his tears he said loudly, without looking at him, "just bloody get going will you Sam. Sometimes you can be a dick, you know that." Then he hung his head and continued to sob softly to himself.

Chapter Six

It took the whole night driving with the good moon until they reached the main north-south highway, over 100 kilometres past the soft sandy patch where George had ripped up the track in his fit of madness, and 80 kilometres past the turnoff to the community up at Warmunya and the various side roads to the outstations closer in. Past there the going was easier until they reached the highway, with the better road at least graded occasionally by someone from government. The days were still very hot and anyway their habit was to take their siesta then, so as they drove on each day they would find some shade to stop and rest the moment it became too uncomfortable for travel.

All the way Obi and Peter talked quietly together, leaving Sam to his own thoughts. Every now and then his ear turned to their conversation and he marveled at how quickly Obi had started to pick up the language. On his own he was further impressed by the way George's truck was handling the rough terrain, wondering that a bushman and prospector of his obvious experience could have come to grief the way he did.

Places are the same but times change. Maybe he had been too good at what he did and found himself in a rut. Stuck in a rut was right, a temporal thing Sam thought to himself, figuratively as well as literally. The one mistake he made, perhaps his only mistake, lay in picking up this real smart kid, who questioned him and made him think, and as probably with his clever mouth got under his skin.

"Alex," he asked suddenly.

"What?"

"What were you and George arguing about when he got bogged?"

"Arguing?" Obi looked ahead out the front windscreen a moment then turned to him. "No, we weren't arguing, Sam. Nothing like that. No, he reckoned he knew these blokes in Queensland who could take the gems off his hands, nudge nudge, wink wink, but I told him he was wrong, he could get a much better price if we went through my Dad's law firm in Melbourne, or maybe Auntie Edie's jewelers. And it would all be kosher, no problem. That's what we were talking about. He reckoned I was up myself, just a smart arse little shit, it was his treasure and he would do what he wanted with it, so I told him he could stick it up his bum."

Obi thought a moment. "That's when he got bogged, after we missed the turnoff."

Thinking further before continuing, he added, "Well, maybe we were arguing. I didn't think we were. He just didn't know what he was talking about, that's all. Why do you want to know?"

Instead of answering Sam chuckled and shook his head, then turned his attention to the road ahead. Presently Obi went back to his unending conversation with Peter and on the hard bitumen now they began to eat up mile after mile.

Toward evening another truck appeared, coming toward them. It began as a small dot on the far horizon, flickering occasionally through the mirage haze, but quickly took shape. As it drew close it slowed. The driver waved them down, so Sam pulled over to the side of the road to wait while the other truck stopped and turned around, then pulled up on the bitumen alongside. Obi glanced anxiously at him.

"G'day mate," a rough voice called as two men looked across. "Thought you might be George. George Summers. That's his truck."

"Was," Sam replied. "He's dead. Snakebite. We're taking his gear down to Tennant Creek, to the police station, then we're off to Adelaide."

"Is that right?" the other said. "How long ago?"

"'Bout three weeks."

The two men glanced at one another.

"Is that all his gear?"

"Haven't touched anything." Sam lied. "Anything here of yours?"

"Nah. Just wondering."

"We'll be off then. See the sergeant if you are down that way, if you want anything."

Sam nodded, and put the truck in gear and drove off without saying anything further. As he picked up speed he glanced in the rear view mirror to see the other truck turn around again and head off in the other direction, where it had been heading. He glanced down at Obi, sitting there beside him staring thoughtfully straight ahead.

"Who are those blokes?" Sam wanted to know.

"George's partners. They had a big blue over in Queensland, before he picked me up. I think they're the fellas he was arguing about selling the gems through, on the black market, that I told him not to. Funny them showing up right now. We were just talking about them, remember, back up the road there, about lunch time."

"Is that right? Do they know who you are? Did you meet them before?"

"No, they don't know anything about me. I don't think so, anyway. Like I said, George picked me up this side of Camooweal, on the road, after his argument with them. Must have been in the pub there. He was still stewed up, pretty pissed off. He'd had a bit to drink, you know."

Sam drove on, himself thoughtfully now. Coming into Tennant Creek late the next morning he pulled off the main street and stopping the truck asked them both to wait there while he went and got some decent clothes for them. If anyone came along they were to sit there and say nothing. He would be back presently. He went to the post office first to withdraw some cash, then without thinking more about it on the way back up the street he went inside the big general store where he purchased two pairs of boys jeans and some new shirts, packets of socks and underpants, and elastic-side boots that looked about the right size.

He took them back to the truck then drove back to the motel out on the highway and booked them a big family room. Taking the boys inside he made them shower and scrub themselves from head to foot, using soap, and when they had dried themselves comb their hair properly and get dressed. Then he did likewise.

All present and correct, he inspected them then back in the truck he drove down the main street to the police station where he introduced himself and explained the situation. Presently a big fat sergeant came out and ushered them into his office from which they emerged several hours later tired and hungry. Not far along the street they found a cafe open, where they ordered a huge t-bone steak each with mushrooms and fresh garden salad from down south, followed by ice cream with chocolate topping and crushed nuts, all washed down with a cup of black tea with plenty of sugar.

Tired as they were, back at the motel it was hard to sleep in the fresh clean sheets and soft beds. After tossing and turning awhile the boys stripped their blankets off the big double bed and spread them on the hard floor, where they curled up and were soon dead to the world. Not much later Sam acknowledged their wisdom and did the same.

Just before ten the next morning, after a hearty breakfast followed by a couple of hours exploring the town, they arrived back at the police station and were promptly escorted next door to the court house. A quickly convened session before the local magistrate found that in consideration of Sam's extensive notes and diagrams showing precise GPS data on the grave site, and further conversation by radio between Tennant Creek police and the local community, George Summers had died by misadventure; cause, snakebite. In the absence of any known or immediate next of kin according to police files, in further consideration of costs incurred in returning the vehicle to Tennant Creek, on receipt of his invoice Samuel Francis Flanagan was granted the right to first option on purchasing the vehicle for a like sum.

With respect to the runaway child Alexander Anthony John Lennox, subject to a medical examination and report he was to remain in the care and control of Samuel Flanagan, who would within the week return him to his home in Melbourne. Obi put his hand up at that, and when ordered to do so he declared that his father would probably be overseas on business and may be difficult to contact. They would call him from Adelaide once they ascertained his whereabouts.

The request was duly noted, then finally as the magistrate began to declare the court closed the sergeant reminded him that there had been a reward of two hundred thousand dollars posted for the boy's safe return, and it was his recommendation that it be paid to Sam Flanagan. Sam protested at that, suggesting that the money should instead be paid to the community who needed it far more than he. After some thought the magistrate replied that in the event he was free to dispose of the money as he saw fit, then promptly rose and they all stood as he left the courtroom.

Outside on the street the sergeant shook hands all round and turned and went back to his station, but as Sam started walking on toward the doctor's surgery the boys held back, heads together, so he stopped and waited for them.

Presently Obi came forward and told him quietly, "Sam, listen, I'm not going back to Melbourne."

"Oops!"

"What do you mean, oops?"

"You have to go back. That's your home. That's where your family is."

"I don't have a family. I hate it," Obi insisted, then pleading, "Sam, you have to listen to me. If you make me go back there I will just run away again."

Sam looked around, bewildered. Obi stamped his foot and pushed him off the footpath into a gap between the buildings. He looked up at him, mouth quivering, trying to speak but instead the tears came and he grabbed him around the waist and head tucked into his chest stood there sobbing. Eventually the tears eased, but while he let his arms down he stayed there head-butting him against the wall, holding him there.

"You are being a bastard again, Sam." he said finally. "You just don't get it, do you."

"No, I don't Alex. I know what the girl did, but she won't be there now, will she?"

"Ah, shut up."

He pushed back away from him and stood there glaring, shaking his head. "That's got nothing to do with anything, and you know it. There are always chicks like that. Dad always has them in the house. But just because I got a fuck doesn't make me a bloody delinquent. Shit!"

He turned away at that, and taking Peter by the hand led him over to the truck where together they climbed in and sat without saying anything. Sam strolled thoughtfully down to the cafe where he ordered three big chocolate milkshakes to take away. Climbing up into the truck he passed them around and they sat there awhile sucking straws. All finished he took their cups and starting the truck drove past a bin and threw them in, then turning off the main road drove across to the doctor's surgery indicated by the sergeant.

Inside he handed the paperwork over to the receptionist then sat and waited until Obi was called, then waited a while longer while he was being examined by the doctor. When they were finished he took the envelope from the doctor and drove back to the police station where he handed it over the desk. Leaving the truck parked there in front they walked along the foot path to the travel agents and booked three seats on the afternoon flight to Adelaide.

It was hot, and nothing doing for a few hours they strolled back along the street to the store where he purchased a pair of swimming bathers each, and some towels. Back in the truck they drove out to the town swimming pool where they went through the turnstyle and changed into their bathers, and laughing both boys ran out and jumped with a loud whoop straight into the water. Sam for his part walked quietly around to the shallow end and waded in until the water rose to his chest, then leaned forward and swam freestyle all the way down to the deep end. Surfacing again he looked around but could see neither of them so he began another lap, but as he did so they both dived on him from above. Peter kicked away laughing shyly, but Obi held onto him with both arms around his neck and would not let go.

"I am not going back to Melbourne, Sam. I'm telling you," he said in his ear.

Sam rolled over onto his back, his hand around Obi's stomach making him roll with him and keep his head above water, then paddled with him back to the edge of the pool. One hand on the tiles to steady himself he drew the boy in close and held him. He sighed, then treading water took his head in his free hand and looked him directly in the eye.

"I'm with you, Alex, don't ever think otherwise. But if you want me to do anything for you, you will demonstrate to me that you understand what it means to be courteous and respectful. You were dux of your school, is that correct?"

Obi nodded.

"That tells me you know better than to behave the way you have been lately."

"Sorry," Obi replied after a moment, trying to look away but held there forced to take Sam's steady gaze. It hurt.

"No you are not. There is no such thing. And I will tell you something else, young fellow-my-lad." He paused, looking at him, before asking, "How long before you turn thirteen?"

"Next month."

"And what do think that makes you?"

"A teenager."

"Wrong. I'll tell you something. There is no such thing as a teenager. I will not allow you to use that as an excuse for your bullshit. Already you have forgotten the lesson of the dance. You think now we are back into so-called civilisation suddenly it doesn't matter any more, and you can just go back to behaving any way you feel, treating me like you treat your father, and everyone else probably. Well forget it. If you want to go now, just go, right. You can take the ore-bag, and all the reward money, and just piss off. Go anywhere you want. But if you want to stay with me we play by the rules. That's it."

Obi stared, stunned, his mouth clamped shut and his face pale and taut.

Sam watched him for a moment then nodded. "All right, I thought so."

Then he pulled him in close and held him, speaking softly into his ear while he made no effort to pull away.

"You never had a friend like me, did you, or a brother like Peter, or any of the others."

Obi shook his head slightly, still tense and acutely focused, his eyes distant.

"All right, now we understand one another."

Sam glanced over the boy's shoulder to Peter waiting patiently nearby, then cocked his head and letting Obi go swam directly away to resume his laps up and down the pool.

Soon after a patrol wagon pulled up outside the pool fence and shortly the manager came over and asked Sam to accompany him to the office. One of the duty constables was there to let him know there was a light charter aircraft on the strip ready to return to Adelaide and it could take them as soon as they were ready to go, as a back load. They would organise a refund of his tickets on the commercial run if it suited. He nodded then went out and called the boys over. Quickly they showered and changed leaving their bathers and towels behind for the local Op Shop, or whoever.

Back at the police station they parked the truck in the yard and loaded their gear into the back of the paddy wagon. Sam handed the keys to the sergeant waiting there for them, and as he did so the big man leaned over and passing a packet of medicine to him said the boy had nits and probably worms; the native boy most likely as well, and if he would attend to the matter when they got home the file was closed. As far as he was concerned anyway.

Three hours later they were in a taxi along Wakefield Road and through the city, then east along Kensington before turning off finally into a block of units.

Chapter Seven

Inside Sam's flat the boys stood and gazed around. Obi spied the TV in the corner and went straight across to switch it on. Sam came over and switched it off, indicating their swags and luggage needing to be unpacked, and taking him by the shoulder showed him through to the bathroom and toilet, and finally the spare bedroom. But they were both fidgety and would not be deterred. Back in the small kitchen Obi went over to the fridge and opened the door to find it bare, then turned in askance to Sam.

"There is no food in the place. We'll have to send out for pizza, or Chinese."

"No dinner for you tonight, boys, either of you. That big fat sergeant in Tennant Creek said you have worms, so we are going to have to treat them first."

"Suspected worms. The doctor only said suspected worms, Sam, and had to do some tests to make sure, but he said I was probably all right."

"You gave him a stool sample, didn't you? And a urine sample. Sorry but they came back positive and I have to treat you both straight away." He watched their faces. "You have nits as well, and maybe scabies but I have to check."

"What do you mean?"

"No solids for another twenty four hours. A good dose of senna tonight to clean you out, then worm treatment tomorrow morning."

Obi's mouth dropped and he looked as if he was going to say something rude, but lost the chance.

"You keep telling me I can be a real bastard," Sam interrupted. "Now you are about to find out. First cab off the rank is half a dozen senna tablets, and after you have taken them I want you to drink lots of water, a pint at a time. Then a crew cut for both of you so we can get at the nits, and before you get into the shower a full body check."

He watched their faces closely.

"We can skip the last bit, depends on whether you itch anywhere."

They both looked at one another, shaking their heads.

"No. We don't itch anywhere. Promise."

Peter simply shook his head.

"All right then." Then he looked up and added, seriously, "You need to check yourselves thoroughly with a mirror. Stick it right up your bum if you have to, but give yourselves a good thorough inspection all over, every nook and cranny, and make sure you are not carrying any passengers."

He turned to a small shelf over the sink and taking a pill bottle counted out six senna tablets each and stood watching while they swallowed them one at a time. Then he made them drink two great drafts of water until they could not hold any more. Grabbing both by the shoulder he then steered them down the short passage to their room where he had them strip to their underpants. In the bathroom he sat them one at a time for a clean, close number two crew cut, and sweeping up their long tangled locks left them to shower and change into clean shorts and t-shirt while he doused their nits with kerosene before throwing the lot into the bin.

All cleaned up he allowed them to sit and watch television while he went to bed, quipping with a wry smile that they would not get much sleep tonight anyway. Even then it was not until about two in the morning, after they had dozed on and off for a few hours, that he woke to hear one of them jump up suddenly and run straight down the passage to the toilet. Right after he came back the other repeated the performance, and for the rest of the night between flushing the toilet, draughts of water and cups of peppermint tea to ease their tummy cramps he got what little sleep he could.

Around six just as the sunlight started through the window he rose and went to the kitchen where he started crushing cloves and wormwood in a mortar and pestle, adding a packet of walnuts and lastly for good measure a whole knob of garlic. That done he scraped the mess into the blender and added a cup of olive oil to thin it and make it go down. He took the bowl into the living room and sat spooning it into them. They were too dazed to resist, but screwing up their faces in disgust they nonetheless soon had it finished so he turned off the TV and sent them to clean their teeth and go to bed.

The rest of the day was no more pleasant, and in between attending to the boys Sam rang the university to make appointments later in the week with his academic supervisor, the head of media services, and lastly the Centre for Indigenous Studies. Sitting back thinking awhile, he also made a call to the headmaster of the university's secondary college, and after a brief discussion retired to his study where he unpacked all his journals and field notes. Fumbling around in his camera case his fingers brushed the bag of gold and gems, and on impulse took it out. Absently he spilled the glittering stones onto his desk and fingered through them. He opened the smaller bag full of nuggets and poured them all out onto his open journal, then as abruptly he put everything back and placed the bag carefully in the bottom draw of his desk.

He sighed and stood up, placing his chair neatly under the desk, and went out onto the balcony. It was always like this when he returned. For days on end he was disoriented and confused, having to adjust so radically from one life to the other and back again. He realised that one day he would have to choose between the institution and the desert, but shaking the thought away went and lay down on his bed. He must have dozed off because the light had faded when Obi came in to wake him. He wanted him to come and look at the stuff in the toilet, and when he did saw it was a tapeworm, like a lump of tangled spaghetti there in the bowl.

"Yes, that's the reason for the treatment. Sorry to be rough on you. We had to dislodge it somehow."

The boy simply nodded, then shook his head slowly from side to side in disgust, his face pale and blank.

They flushed it down. Before long Peter took his turn while Obi went and showered again, taking advice this time to inspect his body thoroughly with Sam's shaving mirror. When they were both cleaned and dressed neatly in their baggies and t-shirts he took them down to the city for a look around. They were both quiet and subdued. He didn't blame them, but instead of taking them out to a restaurant dinner as he had thought he might they wanted pizza, and on the way home stopped in at a local bottle shop to select a nice bottle of Barossa red to wash it down. At that point he decided to fly across to Melbourne first thing tomorrow and get the business with Obi sorted out. That particular burden lifted he called in at a video store and let them browse through and select what they wanted.

One glass of wine finished him, however, and soon into the movie he lay back on the couch and nodded off again, waking quite a bit later to find the pizza only half eaten and Obi snuggled against him, sound asleep, with Peter on his other side dead to the world. Carefully he picked one up and carried him to bed, changed him into his pyjamas and tucked him in, then came back for the other and repeated the process before turning in for the night.

Just after eleven o'clock next day they were in Melbourne, heading down the Tullamarine Freeway in a hire car they picked up at the airport. Obi gave him an address in Toorak so they drove on down through Port Melbourne, bypassing the city along the Westgate Freeway and down Kingsway onto Toorak Road. Obi was on his home turf here so Sam listened patiently as he showed him the way. Soon they pulled up in front of a large Federation house set back on manicured lawns bordered with roses. They all sat in the car looking at it a moment.

"Is that your house, Alex?" he wanted to know.

"No, this is Aunty Edie's. We live over there," he said, pointing to another even larger house down the street only a little, just across a slight dogleg in the road.

"Don't you want to go home?"

Obi shook his head, then glared at him a moment before opening his door and stepping out onto the grassy verge. He looked around then hung his head, and after a moment got back into the car and sat there. Sam looked at him curiously.

"You go, Sam, it will be better that way," he said finally. "She won't bite. Just ring the front door bell," he added. "She will be in the front parlour this time of day having her cup of tea."

Sam glanced at him ruefully, then shrugged and stepped out of the car and walked across the verge and up the path to the broad verandah, where he pressed the button briefly and waited. Footsteps approached from inside and the door opened to reveal a thin, slight old lady in a skirt and blouse with a single string of pearls at her throat.

"Sam Flanagan, well bless my soul. What a pleasant surprise." she exclaimed.

He stood there completely at a loss. "Lady Edith," he managed finally. "There must be some mistake."

He took a step back and held his hand up for her to wait, then turning on his heel strode quickly back down the path to the car. He leaned through the open window at Obi.

"Alex, your Aunty Edie doesn't just happen to be Lady Edith Bauer, does she?"

"Yes," he answered, somewhat taken aback as if being made to state the obvious. Then his brow furrowed and he looked at him quizzically. "Do you know her?"

"Of course I know her. Who do you think pays my bills?"

Obi shrugged. "I don't know. How would I know? I mean, I didn't know it was you, maybe somebody like you, doesn't surprise me." He looked up. "That's what I thought, anyway."

Sam stood gazing around for a moment, then leaning forward again said abruptly, "Come on, let's get this show on the road, eh."

Slowly Obi opened the door and stood waiting until Peter got out as well, then pushed him ahead while they followed Sam back up the path to the verandah. When they got there the two of the family looked entirely past one another, so to keep the thing moving Sam introduced Peter to Lady Edith who politely ushered them inside where she sat them all at her little table, and rang a small bell to summon the maid for a fresh pot of tea for her guests.

Having done that she fiddled delicately with her napkin for a moment, and then strangely, as if talking to a spot on the far wall opposite, asked nobody in particular, "Do you have something to say to me?"

Obi appeared about two inches tall, his own eyes staring down the passage toward the dining room.

"Sorry, Aunty," he said eyes wide and glistening, and in such a very small voice it was barely audible. That was all he could manage.

"I should think so." She coughed politely, covering her mouth with a dainty hand. Turning to Sam she added brightly. "Dear me, Dr Flanagan, how silly of us. Where on earth did you find him? You of all people."

"He found us, actually. It is a long story, but he was very brave. I want you to know that."

By then the maid had returned with fresh tea, and Lady Edith leaned over with her hand on her arm asking her to call Jack on the telephone and suggest he come over. She had a surprise for him.

Obi shrank even further into his seat, looking as if he were ready to bolt. It was at that point that Lady Edith looked at him for the first time and held him riveted there with her gaze.

"Come here and let me look at you," she said finally. Standing slowly Obi pushed his chair in and went to stand next to her, eyes not leaving her face. She reached up and touched him lightly on the cheek.

"You have grown a little," she said absently, then more directly, "and you have changed, haven't you."

He nodded. Still holding her hand to his cheek she turned and asked, "What are your plans for him, Sam?"

"My opinion, ma'am," he said bluntly "is that he is better off out of this environment."

"Indeed," she acknowledged, then let him continue.

"His mind needs to be disciplined. I know Melbourne has facilities to cater for his intellect, but his domestic situation provides too much distraction. In Adelaide we can enter him in an accelerated stream into early tertiary entry. There is a senior college on campus that would suit him quite well. I have it in mind that Peter should also attend college with him, where he will receive a great deal of support from our indigenous studies people. The boys have bonded well, and separating them now would not be in their best interest."

She nodded wisely. Obi leaned forward breaking contact with his aunt to interrupt, "Sam, really, how do you know Aunty Edith?"

"Lady Bauer is my research sponsor. We met while I was doing Honours, when she sought my opinion on one of her children's books."

Suddenly Peter glanced up at her, staring intently, and she returned his gaze with a sweet, knowing smile. At that moment she cocked her head and looked at Obi.

"What were you doing on that track, Alexander? You were going the wrong way. How did you get to be there?"

"What? Where? Where George got bogged? That place? No, we missed the turnoff up to the community. He wanted to call in there for news, and get some supplies, but we were arguing and drove right past. That's when he got bogged, because he stopped suddenly and tried to back up, and it took us ages to get out. Then when the snake got him I didn't want to turn around and get bogged again so I just kept driving and driving and driving. It seemed like forever. Next thing I knew Sam had hold of me."

He blurted everything out then stopped suddenly, staring at her, frightened, then away again, and visibly withdrawing back into himself stood silent.

At that point the doorbell rang and the maid went to answer it. She opened the door and Jack Lennox came pacing through to take in the whole gathering at a single glance before the maid offered him a seat, and he went to take it. Sam rose at Edith's prompting and they shook hands. He could see the resemblance. No wonder he and Alex clashed, he thought, they were so very much alike, but he held his counsel and sat back waiting for Edith to speak. The father was as plainly in blind awe of the old lady as the son, and they both sat watching her with the same blank look on their faces.

Apparently oblivious, she motioned Obi back to his seat then turned her attention to the pot of tea and spent the next moments filling their cups and offering sweet biscuits.

"You may continue, Dr. Flanagan," she said finally.

For the next hour they thrashed out the new arrangements for Obi's care and control, saying nothing whatever about his stash of gems but finally agreeing on the reward money being put toward a scholarship fund for indigenous students attending the university senior college, the boy Peter Wilson Napantjarra present here today being the inaugural beneficiary rather than sending him to a state school. The arrangements were to be made directly with the college through Lady Edith's charitable trust, with everything else to remain a private family matter.

Eventually Jack rose to go, pleading a luncheon appointment in the city, and shaking Sam rigorously by the hand strode out the door without looking back. Sam glanced across at Obi who sat entirely expressionless, not even looking after his father as he left the house. Once he had gone Edith rang her little bell and when the maid entered she instructed her to escort her guests across to the big house where Alexander would collect his things, then she rose from her chair and bid them all a good day.

Chapter Eight

The house was enormous. The moment they stepped inside Sam could see the problem. Obi would have had rattling around inside it all his short life. It would finally have driven him to distraction. He glanced down at him a moment but the boy simply shrugged then led the way up the ornate stairway toward the back of the house where he had had a suite of rooms to himself. It only took him twenty minutes or so to pack his clothes, and rummage through the cupboards and drawers for small treasures before taking down all his framed certificates and awards, then without a word or backward glance he took up his heavy suitcase and led the way back down the stairs. At the front door he stopped in front of the maid who stood there weeping softly to herself, lace handkerchief dabbing delicately at her cheeks. Obi put down his case and turning gave her a big hug.

"Thank you so much, Adriana cara," he said quietly, "thank you for everything. I will never forget you. I will write to you, is that all right? Say hello to Gino and Lisabetta for me please, and tell them not to worry."

She nodded, then leaned down and kissed him on both cheeks before pushing him away. He looked at her a moment longer, smiling, then turning away took up his case again and left. Back in the car Sam sat a moment watching him carefully, but he sat looking straight ahead through the front windscreen without moving.

Without turning his head, at length Obi said pointedly, "Just go, Sam. Drive away, all right. Don't think I'm sorry because I am not. I'm glad. All right?"

He nodded and pulled away from the curb. Several blocks later he pulled out onto Toorak Road and merged into the flow of traffic. Back on Kingsway he went to turn left to head back through Port Melbourne but Obi waved him on into the city centre, where they drove around only briefly before he pointed out a parking station, and they drove in.

"Did you bring the stuff?" he wanted to know.

Sam patted his satchel there under his legs, and they got out and walked back up onto the street where he hesitated a moment, then leaned down to speak quietly into Obi's ear.

"I don't think it is a good idea to go see your father's lawyers, Alex," he murmured. "There are some fine gem-cutters in Melbourne, as good as anywhere in Europe. I think we should have a chat with them first; at least get an evaluation."

Obi simply nodded, eyes bright, then took his elbow and drew him along. They only went a few hundred metres before he turned into a tall, graceful Art Deco building and waiting a moment for the elevator, drew them in with him and started pushing buttons. Up on the ninth floor they stepped out into a narrow corridor and he led the way again until they came to a tiny office where he knocked briefly and entered. Inside he pressed a buzzer, then sat in the small foyer to wait.

Picking up on their expression as they watched him, he leaned over and said quietly, "Dad had a formal necklace and tiara made here for my mother. Aunty Edie comes here as well."

Presently a small shutter opened to reveal what looked like a bank teller's grill, where they introduced themselves and explained the reason for their visit. Following a brief discussion he took the bag from his satchel and spilled two or three of the larger sapphires and an opal onto the counter. Almost immediately they heard a click and a faint whir, and a door opened suddenly behind them. Almost as quickly a stooped, balding little man came out and ushered them inside. He introduced himself as Johann Beck, and brushing the samples back into the bag took it with him down a short passage. Setting it on a table in his tiny office he sat. As promptly spilling them all out he expertly sorted through them with deft fingers before taking a small tray to empty the bag of gold nuggets as well.

Presently he looked up, and without hesitation said, "Like this, Mr Flanagan, uncut, for the sapphires, perhaps $15-18.00 a carat. These are good Anakie sapphires, yes? Maybe $18.00, maybe not. The opals, they are Lightning Ridge, about the same, $17.50 per gram. The gold I can pay you, say, $900.00 an ounce. For the lot, in the rough, dirty like this" he shrugged, pursing his lips, "perhaps, $55,000.00."

Sam leaned forward slightly. "Cut and polished?"

The jeweler shrugged again. "I can only guess . . . at wholesale, half a million or more."

Obi studied his face a moment, then leaned forward suddenly and said, "You really don't remember me, do you Mr. Beck?"

He stood and reaching over the desk extended his hand. "Alexander Lennox. You know my father, Jack Lennox, and my great aunt Lady Edith Bauer. I've got a tan now, that's all, and a haircut. We've been away on holiday, in Queensland."

The other's mouth dropped, then he smiled in recognition and standing took the boy's hand and shook it vigorously, nodding his apologies in return.

They both sat down again before Sam leaned over and asked, "If these were all made up into a presentation set, with perhaps some smaller pieces to show it off, how much then?"

The man's eyes lost focus for a moment and went distant. His fingers started rearranging the individual gems into different sets. He set his loupe into his eye and began closely to examine each carefully under his desk lamp, one after the other, then rearranged them all again two or three times before finally sitting back, and taking the loupe from his eye set it down on the desk.

He cocked his head then, and shrugged, "You are asking a very great deal, Dr Flanagan. A job like that would take years. I must find a master jeweler interested in taking it on. And this is pure native gold. It is too soft, butter soft. It must be assayed, and alloyed, before it is suited to making up serious art pieces acceptable to the trade."

He fingered the small piles in front of him.

"One presentation case?" he continued. "No. Not for what you have in mind. Five or six smaller cases at least. The various elements do not match quite well enough. Smaller more modest arrangements would be more affordable."

Obi interrupted. "We have plenty of time. I have to go back to school. How much do you think?"

The jeweler shrugged again. His gaze swept slowly from to one and the other and back again before setting his eyes squarely on the boy's face. "Depending on the market, and the economy, and mood, five or six million."

Obi's face lit up. "All right, what's the deal?"

"Well, in this case I would accept your commission, payable on the sale of each piece, with interest at current bank rates on my investment. I cannot accept equity, for a number of good reasons. I'm sure Dr Flanagan will understand."

"You won't say anything to anyone, will you. Especially don't tell my father if you run into him. Or my Aunt. Mr Flanagan's looking after it, all right. He's helping us with school, Peter and I." He turned to put his hand affectionately on his friend's shoulder.

"You will send a quote at each step? And a progress report?" Sam asked.

"Certainly, of course."

The three looked at each other and nodded. As they watched the cutter carefully weighed the various quantities and took notes, finally writing out a receipt which he handed to Sam, smiling distractedly, almost dreamily to himself. At that they all stood and shook hands, and were promptly shown out with calm assurance that they would soon be in touch.

Down on the street heading back toward the parking station Obi mused, almost to himself, "I wouldn't have thought about that myself, Sam, did you know that?"

"Well, yes, I sort of guessed, to tell the truth," he said, walking on. "You were all hung up on your argument with that cranky bloody Queenslander and stopped using your brain."

But Obi was no longer listening. Sam walked on a way before he realised he was alone, then looked back to see the boys standing there gazing intently through a shop window. He went back to join them and after a while suggested it was still early afternoon, asking what would they like to do next? They simply shrugged, preoccupied now with the shops, so they sauntered along before stopping for a late lunch. Afterward they wandered around taking in the sights before finally driving out to the airport for an evening flight back to Adelaide.

Chapter Nine

Sam was soon to learn that, as one of the prime ministers once said, life was not meant to be easy. Still fidgeting all next morning, after lunch he left the boys to watch television and went out, walking all the way to the university, calling into the department briefly to catch up with the other post-grads. Looking around he found the place empty so he lingered briefly, then almost as an afterthought penned his name on the notice board for a seminar on a topic of classificatory kinship and ritual adoption in the Central Desert. Wandering off campus he made his way slowly back up the main street until an estate agent's window caught his eye, and he stood there awhile browsing the available property rentals.

Back home finally the boys were still there lounging lazily on the couch, with a movie on only partly being watched, and the moment he entered they looked up in askance. Not taking their bait he pottered around in the kitchen making himself a sandwich and a cup of tea, then took his lunch into the living room where he sat on the end of the couch taking in the scraps of movie. Finally he finished and placing his plate on the coffee table sat down in a chair opposite.

Obi watched him a moment then got up and went over to the TV and switched it off, then sat down again a shy grin breaking his face. Sam sat waiting for him to speak, but he looked away suddenly, embarrassed.

Peter sat back somewhat bemused at his expression, then leaned forward and said quietly, "No worry, Sam, we like you. You good fella."

"I'm not worried, just a bit tired. Too much on my plate I guess. What are you boys up to?"

They shrugged, gazing back his way again.

The onus was on him. He stared away, out through the window and across the balcony to the neighbouring houses and backyards, and beyond into the distance.

"We might move house, I think," he said finally, "find a bigger place, before we get too settled. What do you reckon?"

"It's all right here," Obi began to protest.

Sam looked at him. "Well, the thing is, I can't have you sitting there watching television all day. That's the other reason. There are some nice places fairly close by, overlooking the park, and there are playing fields there too. You boys should be out kicking a football, and running around."

Obi didn't say anything to that but Peter picked up noticeably, so when he turned to leave they both got up and scampered after him, laughing and jostling at one another. Like puppies he thought. Maybe he ought to relax; loosen up a bit. Out on the street he picked up on their mood and they walked along together to the real estate office where they looked through the display of apartments for rent before choosing a large three bedroom, open plan affair looking out across the river.

They spent the whole of the next day moving. The boys wanted to share the big master bedroom, with two single beds and two desks aside from the huge walk-in robe, leaving Sam a second bedroom for sleeping and the third which he converted into his study.

There was a car parking bay for them downstairs at ground level, so he tried the new phone to find it worked already and rang through to Tennant Creek to the police station, to have the truck sent down some time on the train. At least they could get out of town occasionally and over the border into western Victoria, to see his parents now and then, which had been a real problem all his undergraduate years while he struggled to make ends meet.

The following day they had an appointment with their new headmaster. The situation was explained to him and after a lengthy discussion about Obi's achievements and what he would like to do next, they turned their attention to Peter. After some delay, finally they patched through to the community by radio. Ten minutes passed while someone went to fetch Bertram, though things being all right by him the teacher had left and her replacement would not be arriving for another two weeks. After more delay they found the previous teacher's telephone number in Glenelg, here in Adelaide. She was mildly annoyed to learn of their whereabouts since she had arranged for Peter to travel south with her when they came back in from the desert, but once everything was explained she was happy with the result. Sam found himself annoyed too, on learning all this, since nobody had told him anything either, but yes, they all agreed university senior college would be very well suited to Peter's capabilities and she would come into town immediately with his record.

The headmaster let them go at that and left them with his secretary. It was well past noon by the time Peter's teacher arrived and they were able to complete the last of the paperwork, and when they finished she asked them if they would like to have lunch.

Strolling back down toward the mall Sam kept glancing her way. She had naturally laughing eyes and a down-to-earth, no nonsense manner about her, and it struck him that she would be a very good teacher. Peter plainly liked her but kept his distance walking ahead all the way with Obi, leaning over occasionally to whisper in his ear while they both giggled. It occurred to him only then why Bertram had sent him south in the truck instead of taking him back up to the community as she had arranged, since he was now a man, no longer a boy. He knew also that she had been adopted into an opposite moiety, making her classificatory wife. He knew that because he had once spent a whole week with the old ladies, mapping all their various kinship categories and who was related to whom, and joking endlessly about the various white staff on the place. It caused him to blush slightly because she was very pretty, and being Peter's tribal brother he realised suddenly how inappropriate was this gathering.

Unable to think of anything else to do, he stopped suddenly and slapped his palm to his forehead. "Ah, Miss Keys, I am begging your pardon," he blurted out. "I completely forgot. I have an appointment with my supervisor at one. Sorry about lunch. Can I give you a ring? About Peter?"

She nodded, disappointed, and he turned on his heels and smiling shyly waved goodbye, with the boys passing her a few paces behind grinning from ear to ear.

Halfway back up the block they caught up with him and running ahead a little turned and burst out laughing. He stopped, bemused, but Peter had sprung him he knew and he was not going to be allowed to get away with it. At once the boy began a dance, there on the street, his hand slapping at his forehead in perfect mimicry, then they both doubled up until tears ran down their cheeks. People were stopping to watch so he turned away and engrossed himself in a window display until they quietened a little, then affectionately cuffing Peter on the side of the head without a word he strode on up the street.

Obi ran up beside him. "Sorry, Sam."

"No you're not, Alex, I've told you that before. I was had, that's all. Peter can be very, very funny. It was very funny and you're still grinning, so saying you're sorry is worse."

"Don't be so grouchy."

He stopped then, but Obi looked up at him thoughtfully and continued, "No, you are just too bloody intellectual, aren't you."

"The day will come when you'll be glad of that. You'd be glad of it already if you had any sense."

Then he walked on, catching Peter at the corner of his eye watching them both intently with those great deep dark pools of eyes of his, but he gave him a wink causing his face to break up in a broad grin. Obi caught the exchange, and taken aback suddenly followed along behind shaking his head in bewilderment.

As they opened the door to their new quarters the phone rang and Sam hurried in to answer it. It was the Tennant Creek police to tell him Sergeant Pierce had sent the truck down the day after they left, and it should be there in Adelaide already. Thanking them he rang the railways and they said yes, it was up at the freight terminal, he could collect it any time. He hung up and noticed both boys watching him so he picked up the phone again and called a taxi to drive them to the railway yards, then motioning them downstairs again and back onto the street they stood there on the verge waiting for it to arrive.

In due course they reached their destination and were dropped off at the big goods shed where after a few tries they finally found the office. Sam paid the freight owing, and on being handed the keys they were directed outside and along to the end of the building. As they stepped off the landing and turned the corner of the shed there were two men at the back of the truck, one on his knees and the other standing gazing around. On their approach the other stood and they both walked off a short way to where a hire car was parked, and looked as if they were going to get into it.

"Those blokes," Obi said quietly, almost to himself, once they had started the truck and begun to drive off. "Up on the highway north of Tennant Creek. They stopped us on the side of the road, thinking you were George, remember?"

Sam glanced down at him, then at the rear view mirror. The car was still there but the men were in it now, watching him drive away. Heading back along the great long building past the office he noticed it beginning to nose around the far end where they had just come. He drove on steady through the big railway marshaling yard and turning onto the main road merged with the traffic.

"Any idea who they are, aside from being in with George?" he asked Obi finally.

He shrugged and shook his head, then out of the blue Peter answered in his place, "Frank Lacy, that one fella, tall skinny fella. No good, that one." He paused, pursing his lips. "'Nother fella, that fat man, 'e Lenny McCarthy."

They drove on a little saying nothing for a while, then Peter started again, "The big one fella, finish up now belong snake, belong this brother

Alecki," he nudged at Obi, "that one, before, that fella Lenny McCarthy work with him, eh. Gem dealer, that mob."

Then he added, pointedly now, "Maybe lookin' for something, boss."

"Well, they won't find anything will they."

Then Obi spoke up finally, vehemently, "Sell the truck, Sam. I've got a bad feeling about this. Just sell it, the whole lot, the way it is."

Sam shrugged. "We need this truck, Alex," he said. "I don't have the money to buy another vehicle, and with you boys we need to get around."

"No, sell it. I have money. My allowance. I never touched my allowance all the time I was away, otherwise they would have checked with the bank and known where I was. Knowing Dad the bank will still be transferring money whether I use the account or not. He's funny like that, always pays his way he says. No, don't worry about money, just sell the truck."

"It is not mine to sell. I don't actually own it yet. I haven't even transferred the registration papers, nothing. There is nothing in my name at all."

The drove along a bit further and suddenly Obi reached forward to open the glove box, and took out a clean sheaf of papers sitting there on top. He started sorting through them.

"There," he said after a brief pause, "that's the receipt from the police. This next one is from the court. Deceased estate it says. That good old sergeant sent everything down with the truck."

Peter leaned forward to see past Obi, watching his face intently for a moment, then leaned back in his seat thoughtfully.

"That's right, boss. Better do what 'e says," he said. "That fella comin' up now, 'e looking at us. That car now, comin' up behind. No good. They bad men, we know that fella. We sell 'im truck now all right. That fella see us sell truck, follow truck. This truck no bloody good, mapun truck this one. Let 'im 'ave it, eh? We go 'nother truck better."

He glanced at them both, then thinking awhile shrugged and shook his head. At the next intersection he turned right off the main road and a few blocks further on drove into a big car yard where after half an hour of bickering and arguing they climbed into a much newer model, set up much the same but without all the extras George had built himself, and drove out again. The other car was back up a side street across the road, the men inside watching them leave.

Chapter Ten

When they returned home it was in a different vehicle from that which Sam had expected to be driving. The boys got out and ran upstairs but as he went to follow them he looked up at the apartment building, which was different too from where he had lived for the past nearly seven years. He walked around the new Landcruiser and kicked the tires, then sighed and taking a deep breath went straight up the stairs.

Safely ensconced in his new study he switched on the computer. As the screen flickered on and system fired up he took his big camera from its case and began sorting through the stock of mini DV tapes recording that last field trip. Logging into the system, he then ran the long firewire cable from the camera to the computer and began capturing and archiving the raw footage. As each tape was processed he switched the camera off and replaced it with the next, repeating the operation until he was finished. That job done he backed up the entire archive onto a big external drive, and for good measure finally burned each film onto DVD which he carefully labeled and set aside.

The work was good. He was very happy with it. The extra year he had spent in the media lab was a good investment. At length he settled down to skimming through each sequence, stopping occasionally to view various sections before fast-forwarding to the next. Absently he turned the speakers on with the sound down a little so as to take in the rhythmic beat while he absorbed the dance. Soon became so engrossed he failed to notice the two boys come in and stand there quietly looking over his shoulder. He didn't realise they were there until he pushed his chair back ready to rise, and a wheel caught Obi's foot causing him to cry out. He jumped, startled, then cuffing them both went out into the kitchen to make himself another cup of tea and a sandwich.

They followed him out and stood there as quietly, watching him with interest.

"What did you think of that, Master Jedi?" he asked without turning, busying himself with the kettle, then cups down from the cupboard.

"Well, I know Edie, she doesn't waste money. But this is hell good, Sam. I never thought your camera was that good."

"Now you know, eh?"

"Yep." Obi paused. "And thanks for saving my life. I haven't thanked you for that yet, have I?"

"Ah, well, it was close enough, that's a fact. A few more hours like that, once the sun came up, and you wouldn't be here now." Sam paused thoughtfully, looking the boy up and down, then shook his head. "No, mate, your Jedi training is what saved you, truth be known. That's where your head was. That's what you were burbling about."

Then he turned to him seriously. "Don't say any more about it, deal? Right now we have better things to be doing. I have to get those pilots ready for my supervisor tomorrow, then some of the footage of Peter for our media people."

"And you, Alex, you don't mind do you?" he added suddenly, excited now. "That sequence with you and Peter is stunning. I would like to use that as well."

"Sure, use what you want. Why would I mind?"

"Because the sequence is uninhibited, it's full frontal. I am sorry I was lost in the dance and kept the camera running all the way through. It hasn't been okayed yet. I'll have to get clearance from my ethics committee."

"Nobody had any clothes on, Sam." Obi objected, "You know that. Only body painting, and dick tassels and feathers, but it was totemic not just for decoration. It was great, really something." Obi picked up on his earlier excitement. "It was really important. The colours and the light were wicked, and the stage setting was fantastic. You're not looking at it right."

He paused then, curious, "anyway, why am I so different? Because I'm a white boy? Boys are all the same. Why would I get into trouble for that?"

"No, not you, me," Sam corrected him. "It might raise eyebrows, that's all. No, forget it. We'll be right. Come and help if you like, let me know if you want anything cut in particular, anything you don't want people to see."

The boys stared oddly at him, as Obi stammered, "What? That part doesn't matter, that's not the crucial part. That's only the dance bit at the end. Anyone can see that."

"What do you mean?"

"Up the back, behind the big hill there where they kill the boys and make them into men, before the big dancing starts. That's what you aren't allowed to see, Sam. Don't you know?"

Obi paused, thinking, then looked up again.

"In Tennant Creek, you said something to me about remembering the dance. I am not a boy any more. Do you remember? In the swimming pool?" He stopped abruptly, cocking his head. "But that's not it. You don't get it. They don't tell you much, do they?"

Peter nudged him to stop while Sam gaped at them before turning sharply away.

"Damn!"

The boys glanced at one another before Obi continued. "You have to get permission from Dobby, Sam. You know, old Dobby, Bertram's father-in-law. He's Peter's grandfather on his mother's side. Not Vincent, Dobby. He's not the same mob; different skin. Of course you know him. You just never talk to him much."

Sam shook his head, thoroughly frustrated, angry now. "Well, all right, bugger it! Look, wait until I make some lunch and you can help me edit the dance sequences. At least we have something to show."

He should not have said that, not there in the kitchen at any rate, because the moment it left his mouth the two of them were off running and jostling back through to his study and onto his chair. They scrambled arguing for control then after a moment sat, confused, waiting for him to arrive. When he came in finally with his tea and sandwiches he chuckled to see them there so earnestly, breaking his dark mood, so he took another chair and sat just behind them.

For the next half hour he showed them the various controls; how to set 'in' and 'out' points and drag each sequence across to the monitor window, into their final footage. Backtracking from there he sat and began explaining the fundamentals of scripting, and what they hoped to achieve with the film they wanted to produce, but they soon lost patience with him and turned their attention instead to the big HD TV camera. He stopped them, promising they could use the small hand-held camera sometime if they wanted to practice, but right now they needed to get this rough cut done for tomorrow.

He sat back awhile, thinking they would be starting school next week and wouldn't that be great, but as he watched them work he found himself intrigued by the pieces of dance they were selecting, and in particular Peter's exquisite timing. He leaned forward again and picking up his diary began to take notes, engaging small talk with them to test their response, then slowly to a full inquisition while their attention was focused so well on the dance sequences; on what they were thinking about as they viewed the footage and why did they cut there, at that point, and not back a little or forward. At times Peter answered excitedly in language, but gently Sam coaxed him back into his outback pidgin and had him pause as he wrote before starting him explaining the next dance steps as he came to them. He watched Obi closely, taking his cue from him as much as Peter, then finally something he said caught his attention and he pulled him up on it.

"What did you just say?"

"What?"

"You, Alex, what did you just say?"

"Ah, I was just talking about all those old brothers, that we call father mob, the way they are together."

"What about them?"

"They would die for each other, you know that? They would die to protect us, as well. The white people don't have anything like that. Just a bunch of shits. My brother would never look after me like that. Not Peter, my real brother I mean, my brother Sam. Him and Mum, and her bunch of friends, arty-farty so-called friends, they just don't get it."

Sam stared blankly at him, and Peter backed away a little while Obi gradually sensed the changed atmosphere. Realising what he had let out his face froze into a mask, but his eyes still glittered dark pools, deep, flashing and angry.

"Yeah, she's still alive. She didn't die like I said. She never had cancer, but she might as well. Fucking brain cancer. Shit! And I'm not sorry. It's like she's dead. Her and Sam. They can get fucked."

"She didn't want me," he paused and went on. "She tried to have me aborted, and Sam never let me forget it. He's fucking evil. He wouldn't leave me alone either, when I was little, but at least Ysabella was fun."

"Alex," Sam stopped him. "What are you saying, that you have a brother Sam; an older brother, who molested you? And your mother knew? You're talking about your own mother."

Obi returned his gaze, steady, unmoving.

"No." he said. "Shut up, I didn't say anything. Nanna looked after me, that's all, then when she died Aunty Edie helped raise me, she and Adriana. She tried her best. And Dad, you know. He's all right, just busy all the time. Maybe he's so busy . . . . . he's like me at lot . . . . . I really worked hard at school, and I studied Jedi, you know that too . . . . . I studied Zen . . . . . really . . . . . everything I could get my hands on . . . . . . no, I don't want to talk about it. It's just not real. What's real? It's just a bad dream I had, Sam."

He leaned toward Peter and put his arm around him. "This is my brother. And you. You're not gay, you're real. You're my mates, and my family. You're what I've got. It was meant to be this way. Shut up about it, all right."

He glared, challenging them, then turned back to editing the film. The sequence had run on and he had to rewind and set a new 'out' point before he could continue. Eventually the work was finished. It was dusk outside, but Sam found himself awed with the result and showed them finally how to burn their work to DVD. That done he packed up and took them down to the city for Chinese.

There was another boy there at the takeaway counter when they came in off the street, and the two greeted him. He was a little older, thirteen or fourteen, scrawny but obviously past puberty, with a slight furry moustache on his top lip and curly red hair standing straight up off his scalp.

"Who's that?" Sam wanted to know.

"That's Patrick. He's in our class. Going to be, anyway."

Obi reached over and grabbed Patrick's arm, pulling him in close. After introducing him to Sam they went to sit down so he changed his order to theirs and joined them.

The meal was quiet. Nobody said much. Sam and Peter kept glancing across at Obi until Sam said softly to him, "Alex, you really can't leave things like that with someone like your own mother. You can't just walk away leaving those sorts of loose ends. We still have a few days, why don't we fly over to Melbourne and see if we can sort it out?"

Obi froze, then turned to chatter with Patrick but the other two held their attention so the other boy shyly demurred.

"You're not going to let it go, are you?" he demanded.

"No." Sam shook his head, and Peter followed suit.

He looked out the window, gazing momentarily at the passing traffic.

"All right," he said eventually. "You'll see. Don't say later I didn't tell you."

Chapter Eleven

Obi dodged his way through the traffic, skirting the busy inside lane to skip across to the tram stop straddling the middle of the road. Sam and Peter were left behind on the kerb, Peter jammed between a fat lady burdened with shopping bags and a begowned lawyer trundling a black document case on plastic wheels. Rather than wait for them he darted over to the other side, then turned to watch as they carefully negotiated the stream of cars and trucks.

"You're being a shit, Alex," Sam said when they finally caught up.

"It was your idea. I told you, but you don't listen," Obi glared back at him accusingly.

"All right." Sam took a deep breath. "Where next?"

"Just down the next lane," Obi pointed, then turned away and started off again, "around that corner where the antique shop is, then through that arcade along there. Come on, I'll show you."

Off the street it was quiet and subdued, the stained glass high up in the arcade ceiling creating a strange effect down here at ground level. Obi quietened his pace and fell in beside Peter, until as they approached a somewhat plain, minimalist shop-front identified only by an engraved plaque he began to straggle. Sam stopped to check with him, but he only shrugged. There was a long pause while he studiously avoided Sam's gaze, then stepping forward suddenly shoved them both abruptly through the door.

The long narrow gallery was deserted. Soft spots of light illuminated vibrant canvas along walls painted in a neutral creamy vanilla, sufficiently off-white to complement the paintings but not allowing any intrusion upon the moment of each piece there under its own lamp. Sam and Peter wandered toward the back of the shop while Obi lingered near the door, making his way thoughtfully from one canvas to the next.

After a while a door slammed somewhere out the back, and a clutter was heard of cups and a kettle whistling.

"Andrea! Andrea, darling," a woman's voice called.

No answer came, until after a moment a head and half a body popped out from behind a partition and she saw Sam and Peter nearby looking at one of the paintings.

"Oh! Terribly sorry! Just ducked out for a moment. Would you like coffee?"

"No, not for me, thanks," Sam replied, smiling.

"Wine? I have a nice unwooded Chardonnay. Just the thing for after lunch. And a soft drink for your boy? A native boy. Such a good looking boy, my." She paused, looking Peter curiously up and down. "Orange juice perhaps?"

"Yes, why not?" Sam offered.

She disappeared, and after a minute came out carrying a tray bearing two glasses of white wine that sparkled in the spots of light, and a can of Fanta. Peter began to say there should be two Fantas, not one, but the woman had already stopped in her tracks. Her fixed gaze drew their attention to Obi still there at the front of the shop. He had taken two paintings down and was rearranging them.

"They are abstract, Alexander. Put them right back the way they were," she said coldly.

"No, darling," he replied. "It's a semi-impressionist triptych and has to be viewed from an oblique angle. The experience is surreal. You walk past, don't you know, not stand in front. The view shifts. It flows. Very clever, really. You had them hung as three separate pieces," he paused critically, "and they are out of order."

He rehung them, then stepped back. After a moment he stepped to one side for another view. Nodding to himself he stepped over to the other side and looked again.

Sam watched him, fascinated, trying to suppress a grin. "Cheeky little bugger," he thought.

The boy was right of course, the colours did swirl, gay and capricious, but it was pure chance. They were three different paintings.

"There, you see, darling. So very casual. Just the thing for informal dining," Obi continued with his patter, plum in mouth. He waited but she refused to budge, so he started toward her.

She swung on her heel as her son approached and returned the tray to the small kitchen alcove at the rear of the gallery, then came back to stand fully before them one arm across her bosom with her other hand enquiringly to her cheek.

"Who are you people?" she demanded.

"Mrs Lennox, my apologies, we haven't had a chance to introduce ourselves," Sam began. "My name is Sam Flanagan, and I . . . . "

"The anthropologist, is it?" challenging him. "You are he, who corrupted my son. You dare to enter my gallery?"

"Well, of course. Why not? He's not corrupt, whatever that means. We thought maybe you and he could make up, be friends."

"Sam, I told you it wouldn't work." Obi was nearby, not letting go.

She backed away, threatened by the three male figures, until the rear door banged again and another woman appeared from the small kitchen and stood taking in the scene.

"Hello Andrea," Obi broke the silence, smiling, seeming in control now.

"Alexander. What are you doing here?" She looked about her, frowning, confused for a moment. "Maggie, is everything all right?"

The back door slammed shut again, and a tall, pimply, gangling youth came in. He stopped behind Andrea.

"Sam," Obi moved forward again slightly, "this is my brother Sam. Sam, this is Sam." He turned to his gawky brother adding dryly, "Sam and Sam. Two Sams."

"That is quite enough!" Maggie burst out. "Please leave, all of you, or I shall call the police."

"No you won't, mother."

"No Alexander," Andrea said, her voice frost, "but I will. Sam, be a dear and get my phone from my bag."

Obi started on her but at that Peter turned and grabbed his arm, swinging him away. He stumbled back a few steps but the other leaned into him pushing sideways with his full body length, hips and shoulders, speaking quietly into his ear, then taking him by both shoulders marched him toward the front door.

At the back of the shop his older brother stepped forward defensively, taking his mother by the arm while Sam mumbled his apologies then turned on his heel and followed the two boys.

Obi had pushed Peter away and wandered off to stand by himself in front of the decorated shop window opposite. Sam went across to him but he pushed him away as well, before wandering aimlessly it seemed down the arcade to stop before another shop. He bent his head forward and leaned against the glass, then swung around to glare at them, tears streaming down his cheeks, before turning his back on them to hide his face in a corner between two adjoining doorways.

People were sauntering along the arcade in both directions, glancing at him briefly before moving on. The light dappled from the stained glass high above, mixing the colours. It was difficult getting to him through the milling crowd and confusion, so Sam and Peter just stood helplessly. The other Sam with Andrea came out of the gallery momentarily to see them still there, but disappeared quickly inside just as Obi turned again to his friends.

"Ah, fuck it! Fuck fuck fuck fuck fuck!"

Sam looked down at Peter and shrugged. They walked off leaving Obi behind. Outside the arcade on the busy street he tagged along at a distance, making out he was window-shopping but starting off again the moment they walked on.

They paused to wait only a little as he came close before moving off, playing with him, until eventually he called after them, "That's the wrong bloody way, anyway. Spencer Street is back down there to your right."

Chapter Twelve

The flight back to Adelaide was subdued. There was nothing much to say, and when Sam broached the subject of their trip both boys gazed blankly at him. He watched the way Peter kept Obi's attention, talking to him constantly and pointing things out to him, telling him stories in his soft boy's voice not yet cracked or uneven; never once allowing him to sink back into himself.

The moment they were home the boys went and showered while Sam warmed some cold pizza from the fridge and poured himself a beer. When they came in dressed in pyjamas Obi went to the cupboard and took a glass, then sat at the table where he reached over and poured himself a small beer from Sam's stubby.

"Not too much, Alex," Sam warned. "Just that one, all right?"

Sam watched him closely, however, thinking it may be better if the beer loosened him up, and when he finished his pizza and reached for another he didn't say anything, merely took the bottle and drained the last of it into his own glass before putting it in the bin.

Peter sized up the situation and took himself off to bed without saying anything. It can't have been easy for him either, Sam thought. He turned back to Obi sitting there at the table, but nothing doing he began to tidy the kitchen. Obi promptly went to the fridge and took out another stubby, not saying anything or glancing in Sam's direction, but politely filled his glass first before pouring himself another.

Sam watched him. Communication being established, he thought, then picked up his glass to tilt it slightly toward Obi before taking another sip.

"Cheers," he said softly.

Obi tilted his glass back but said nothing, just sipped his beer slowly while gazing off into the distance.

"Do you want to tell me about your brother?"

"No."

"Do you have a reason?"

"No, not really. He's a bastard, that's all. Different planet. Sleezeville"

Obi watched Sam for a reaction but none came. After a pause he added, "Did you ever read Lord of the Rings? Tolkien?"

"Yes, of course."

"Worm Tongue. That's my brother. You know the rest. Stop talking about it."

Sam looked across at him a moment and nodded, then asked, "So who's Andrea?"

"She's a fucking dyke. Mum's protector. Both of them, Sam and her, got their hooks into her. They want in on Edie's money, that's all."

"Doesn't the gallery make any money?"

"Ha! Bullshit! You saw it. It's all bullshit, just for show, pretending she's not living off Dad's allowance. Mum wouldn't know the bloody Heidelberg School from Dada."

His vehemence struck a chord, and Sam pricked up.

"And you do?"

"Yes I bloody do. You know I do. That gallery space could be keeping four or five good artists. Everyone says. Even Dad says. And you're the expert. Mum's scared of you. If Edie wasn't looking after you there'd be a restraining order against you."

"Me? Me? It has nothing to do with me. What are you talking about?"

"Nothing, they're just scared of you Sam, that's all. Don't worry about it, Edie has it all sorted."

After a pause Obi added thoughtfully, "Well anyway, they don't know anything about the sapphires. Don't say anything, all right?"

Sam sighed. He reached over and took Obi's half full glass and tipped it down the sink, then downed his own before turning his back to rinse both glasses and leave them to drain.

"Go to bed. That's enough. I'm sorry I misjudged the situation, but Peter will say the same thing. We are just not used to your sort of family, all right. Better for you to stay away from them yourself while we get you settled. You have your own life to live, mate."

"That's all I bloody said, Sam. It was you who didn't listen. I don't need them, any of them. Only Edie, because she's good and helps people, but they can have the money I don't want it. I'll make my own money, or not. Maybe I'll be poor instead. It's not worth it, all that crap all the time . . . "

"That's enough! You're better than that, Alex. Much better. Just . . . . learn to fucking shut up sometimes . . . . cut the crap yourself, eh? . . . . semi-impressionist fucking triptych . . . . I never heard so much bullshit . . . ."

Sam stopped abruptly, shaking his head, but stood his ground.

"That's what they're bloody like!" Obi wanted to argue. "They're all like that! Everybody! You saw . . . ."

"Yeah? What's that make you then? Eh? Why don't you just cut the fucking pretense all the time. You're just as bad, trying to be such big shot, all the fucking time! Just be a kid for a bloody change, will ya? Give yourself a fucking break, eh? Taking on all this stuff, you're too young, mate . . . way too young." Sam shook his head in disbelief. "It's not so bad . . . . you've plenty of talent, really, you're very talented, you don't need to bung it on, just . . . . . let go, let yourself be a kid . . . . finally. Be yourself, right. It'll all happen anyway, won't it, without all that argey fuckin' bargey all the time."

Obi started, then hung his head and started crying again. He went on, sobbing quietly to himself, so Sam waited, allowing him space.

"What?" he asked finally.

"Well, just for a start, first you bloody tell me I can't be a teenager I have to be a young man, now you tell me to just be a kid. Then you tell me I'm bright, but act dumb . . . "

"Ah, Jesus Christ! Come here, mate," he said, and Obi stood and came around the table into his arms. Sam held him close, letting him sob, letting his frustration ebb, until eventually Obi dropped his arms and simply leaned against him head-butted into his chest.

"You poor little bugger, you don't know the difference, do you? You never had anyone to play with, just running around and having fun; nobody to sit and talk to. It's been all work, trying to keep up, trying to show everyone you can do it; trying to prove who you are . . . . I mean, it's just not healthy."

He paused thoughtfully, looking down at Obi holding onto him now. He shook his head trying to loose his thoughts, but that didn't work either.

"Go to bed now, Alex. OK?" he said eventually. "We can worry about it tomorrow."

"Can I sleep with you?" Obi asked in a small voice.

"What? Yeah, sure, if you want."

"You won't think I'm gay, or anything like that?"

"Gay? No I don't think you're bloody gay. I really don't care. So long as you don't wake up and mistake me for the lovely Ysabella, I don't give a shit what you are."

"Hardly. Bloody hell, you're way too ugly. And you fart, and you talk in your sleep." Obi looked up, searching. "And it's not what I am. That's not what I meant."

Sam studied his face intently. "It's OK, I like you too. Maybe it's time you learned to say it, when you love someone, and not be ashamed. I'm sorry about what happened to you, but now we've all had this catharsis you can let it go, eh? Just have some fun, relax, eh?"

Obi blushed and looked away, then glanced back sharply.

"Anyway, what about Peter?" he said finally. "He won't sleep if I'm not there."

"All right, him too. But I want you in bed now, got it?"

"Yep."

Obi tore away, turning briefly at the door to look back at him before disappearing.

Sam turned back to the sink shaking his head. He leaned against it for a moment thinking, listening to the two boys thump and jostle down the corridor to his room. As they went quiet, with a sigh he went to the fridge and reaching into the back took a tall bottle of the good local stout he kept, in preference to another stubby from the cheap six-pack of pilsener, then a pint stein from the rack above the sink. He turned and sat at the table. Drawing another chair close he put his feet up and drew the full pint before sitting back to watch the froth settle. Finally he reached over and picking it up by the handle took a good deep draught.

He sat there for over an hour quietly mellowing, the effect of his nectar as he called it letting his mind wander, hazy, unfocussed; his thoughts waxing and waning aimlessly until he rose finally and staggered only slightly to the bathroom where he stripped and showered. The water was hot initially, but he turned the tap down and let the increasingly cold shower prickle at his senses and bring him back from the induced reverie. Dried and with a towel around him he made his way to his bedroom where the boys were entwined on the big bed like pups, sheets and blankets in disarray, dead to the world.

Changed into his pyjamas he went to work to straighten them out and remake the bed, then turning Peter over rolled him to the other side. Obi murmured softly in the midst of some dream or other as he rolled him in turn into the middle snug against Peter. He sat on the edge of the bed watching them both before leaning over to brush Obi's forehead with his thumb, which had the opposite effect from what he intended as he rolled right back on to his side of the bed. He watched him sleeping soundly there a while longer, then with a shrug gave up and went back down the passage to their room where he tucked himself into Obi's bed.

Next morning they were both up with the dawn. Woken by the early morning sun through the window, Sam looked up to see them both sitting there on Peter's bed watching him.

Chapter Thirteen

When he got back on Monday it was late afternoon. The boys were already home. In the kitchen Patrick was sitting there at the table with them going through Obi's collection of way out 1970s comics. They had Bob Dylan playing, and Sam stopped to listen.

"*Highway 61*," he exclaimed. "Great album. Is that yours, Patrick."

"Yeah. *Revisited*, 1965. You like Dylan?"

"Yes, great vocalist, lyrics, he's an icon. You look a bit like him, or Woody Allen maybe."

"Ah, yeah, cultivated image," Patrick chuckled, pleased with himself.

"How are you boys? What's happening?" Sam asked the others.

"Nothing," Obi replied, while Peter sat shyly not saying anything. "Can Patrick stay for dinner?"

"Well, depends. Have you asked his parents? Do they know he's here?"

"Ah, he's boarding at college. Food's terrible. Say yes, Sam."

"Is that right? Do you have leave to be here, mate? Do you have a leave pass?"

"No, not really." He paused. "It's cool, didn't run. Be back in time for dinner. What?"

Sam looked sharply at him and sighed, then at the other two. "OK, just tell me their phone number. I'd better ring and let them know where you are."

"Sam," Obi insisted, if you're ringing them anyway, can he stay for dinner? Don't worry, it'll be all right."

"Yes, all right, just this once. Since you're all new, and so long as it's OK with the college."

He rang though and reported Patrick's whereabouts, promising to return him by eight, then turned back to chastise Obi. "Little bugger you are, this is not a kid's game! Play by the rules, all right!"

The boy was taken aback, but recovered quickly and got up to clear the table. He didn't say anything, just glanced quickly at Sam before disappearing into his room.

"Ain't his fault," Patrick said quietly. "Just talking, yeah. The time, sorta, went."

Sam looked at him.

"It's OK. Don't worry about it. I know you from somewhere. Kid like you. You stand out."

"Paper," Obi said from the door. "His picture was in the paper. His Dad was convicted of lying to some Royal Commission or something. Big Labor politician."

"Ah, yes, that's right." He looked at Patrick again, studying his reaction. "How did you feel about that? Pretty embarrassing, eh?"

"Nah! They embarrassed, not us. Farcical, yeah. Someone to hang by the neck, so they wave their hands in the air and look real moral and upright citizenry. We got a fine, twelve grand, but already cost a hundred. Hell knows the taxpayer. Half a mill, for sure."

Sam nodded, almost to himself, glancing from one boy to the next. "What on earth have I got on my hands? An alternative Prime Minister waiting in the wings, a Permanent Head of Aboriginal Affairs, if we ever get that far, and what about you, Alex? Foreign Affairs? Why me?"

"Because you're such a hell cool dude, Sam. You care." Obi smiled. "You're out there, on the edge of the world, unlimited. Anything's possible."

He paused, watching, "but you're gonna have to get up so we can set the table."

He got out of their way. Deciding against any more work for the day he went to his room and cleaned out his briefcase before tidying the desk, then stripped for a shower. As he came back along the passage with a towel around him the bathroom door was locked.

"All right! Who's locked the bathroom?"

"Ah, that's Patrick. He had to take a slash. He's a bit shy." Obi called from the kitchen.

"Patrick, no locked doors in the house, right?"

The toilet flushed and after a moment the door opened. Patrick come out into the passage and ducked under his arm, glancing up at him in disdain. He followed him into the kitchen to be met by Obi, standing there with a packet of chops from the fridge.

"He doesn't do sleepovers either. Family are strict Catholics."

"I suppose he's vegetarian too, is he?"

"You vegetarian?" Obi wanted to know, but Patrick simply shook his head. Peter sat back grinning from ear to ear.

"No, he's a carnivore, like us. All right? Leave him alone, OK?"

After dinner they went down to the city before strolling back up to Patrick's college just off the main campus. Peter became edgy along the way, fretting and worrying, looking constantly back over his shoulder, occasionally turning around to walk backwards while scanning the street, until Sam stopped as well. Obi and Patrick walked on, lost in their conversation.

"What's up?"

"Something happening, boss," Peter said quietly. "Those fellas there, look. That car there. Down there, look. Down that street, yah? Following us."

Sam searched intently but saw nothing. What can they do? It's the middle of the city, he thought to himself. He turned and walked on, replying out loud, "Ah, I don't think they'll do anything. What would they want from us?"

Peter said nothing more, but stepped up and followed on close beside him. Quickly they caught the other two. When they arrived at the front gate Obi turned and said he wanted to go in with Patrick and borrow *Dharma Bums*.

"*Dharma Bums*?" Sam joshed. "Thought you were a Jedi knight. Jack Kerouak didn't know anything about Taoism. His was a seriously 1950s, post-war, beat sort of Zen. He died young from too much grog. *On The Road* tells you a lot more about Kerouak, about that generation, if that's what you're looking for. He was from Quebec, not Saigon . . . . . he was Jean Louis de Kerouak, from a big family of Quebecois intellectuals. They weren't Buddhist either, not by a long shot. They were only working in the US at that time. He started writing in French, on this long scroll he pasted together . . . "

"Yeah, all right smarty pants, don't give us a lecture."

"Got *On The Road* too," Patrick said. "Wannit?"

"Yep. Wait here a minute," Obi turned to Sam. "I'll be back."

But he wasn't back. While they waited Peter fidgeted, eyes bright and ears turned to every small noise. His gazed turned intently to the college grounds, through the dark and the trees, holding still like a dog pointing game and saying nothing. Fifteen minutes went by, until Sam broke the spell and they went down the long path through overhanging shrubbery to the front door of the college itself, and went inside. Sam rang the little bell at the reception desk and one of the house tutors doing double duty came out.

"Sorry to disturb you. One of my boys came in here about fifteen minutes ago with Patrick Millhouse. He was only supposed to come in to pick up some books and straight out again."

"Oh, really? No, he left. A good ten minutes. Straight out that door."

"You sure?"

"Yes, I am certain. He said he would return Patrick's books next week. He made a point of it, then rushed out with his nose in his book. Jack Kerouak's *Dharma Bums*. For a moment I thought he would bump into the door."

Sam looked suddenly down at Peter, standing there with his back to the counter, frozen like a setter. "What is it, Peter? What's happening?"

"Frank Lacy. That fella took 'im, eh? Those two fellas waiting. They following us, wait for that little brother, then took 'im."

"What?" Sam turned to the night caretaker. "Excuse me, can we borrow a torch? Seems to be some trouble. We think Alex might in trouble."

Quickly a torch was found and they went outside, shining the beam along the edges of the path as they went. Straight away Peter's keen gaze found the book open on its back under a bush. The other book was on the lawn just off the path, and as they followed that direction he bent over and picked up a handkerchief folded into a pad. Sam took it, and with a quick sniff held it back at arms length.

"Chloroform! Shit!"

They fanned out from there, across the lawn and around the back of the building, but it was too late. If they were in a car it had already gone.

"Call the police," Sam turned to the caretaker. "We think he has been abducted."

"No police," Peter interrupted, excited now. "No good. Bugger up everything. We find 'im, no worries. They gone Territory side, lookin' for gemstones, you bet."

"Really? You know all that?" Sam queried.

"Too right. No worries, boss. You ring 'im mission 'ouse, all right. All that mob, Bertram, everybody, find that fella straight away. They going there, heading that way, heading north. We better go now, all right. Go straight away. We chase 'im, take 'im Toyota, find 'im pretty quick."

Sam stopped. Hell, everything falling apart again, he thought. What the bloody hell next? Peter's right, he thought, police won't be any good, they won't believe it. He had already run away once and caused a major search effort. It must have cost thousands. But then he caught Peter's anxiety, another side of him. He was right. Alex is our brother, and we were supposed to have been looking after him. It's important. We had let everybody down.

"All right, don't worry," he said out loud. "We know where he might be. We'll call them from there if we need to."

Chapter Fourteen

Obi woke in a groggy haze, slipping in and out of a bad dream. He became vaguely aware that he was in a truck, on the front seat, propped against somebody or something, then leaned forward slightly and vomited his heart out. In the midst of it he was shoved to one side, but immediately felt a hand on the other shoulder steadying him.

"Fuck. What the fuck!" He heard a gruff voice vaguely.

"Ah, just get the fucking bucket. Give it to him, eh. Here, son, spew into the bucket if yer have ta . . . ."

But at that moment he lapsed back into unconsciousness.

It was just coming on first light when he became more fully awake, still dazed. The road ahead stretched to the horizon, and he thought for a moment he was in the Landcruiser with Sam and Peter. It was the same truck, but they'd sold it. Hadn't they? They had a new truck. Newer, anyway. George. Was it George. But he died. They buried him. There was a smell of vomit and he gagged. A bucket appeared in his lap and he clasped it to him while his stomach emptied itself, then sat back groaning.

Eventually they pulled off the main road onto a side track and drove down it a short way, around a couple of bends, out of sight.

The bloke on the passenger side got out, swearing and cursing. He went to the back of the truck and took down his swag, then proceeded to strip his soiled trousers and pull on a clean pair. The other took the bucket and emptied it before rinsing it clean from one of the water tanks under the tray.

"Come 'ere, yer fuckin' little shit," he called to Obi, who obediently stepped down from the cab.

He stood there quietly, blinking in the soft dawn light trying to clear his head. He stalled, trying to reorient himself, and think what might have happened. He was out the door with Patrick's books when he was tipped over suddenly onto the lawn, something wet over his face. That was it. He felt terrible. His stomach still heaved, but his vision cleared enough to see the two men there watching him. One leaned against the truck gazing steadily at him, while the other short fat guy pranced and hopped, shaping up, looking as if he were going to belt him any minute. He didn't move but stayed swaying slightly, until the tall one stepped forward suddenly.

"All right, enough bullshit. Where are they?"

"What?"

"The sapphires."

"What?"

The fat bloke reached in and slapped Obi hard on the side of the head, knocking him to the ground, but the other stopped him.

"That'll fuckin' do, Lenny. I don't want him marked."

"Ah, you'll be wastin' yer time, Frank. Better just kick the shit out of 'im. Fuck 'im. He'll talk quick enough."

Frank stepped sideways and punched Lenny hard in the jaw with a sharp left jab, then a right to the face, bloodying his nose. He pushed him away, then turned and knelt down next to Obi, still on his hands and knees on the ground.

"Don't fuck me around, cunt. Just tell me where the sapphires are and we'll drop you back home, right. No problems, eh?"

"I don't know what you're talking about," Obi managed finally.

"Cut the crap, eh? We know you were with George, and we know George. He never trusted no-one, not even the bank. He kept everything on him. But he could never help big-notin' himself, showin' off. Lettin' on, always lettin' on, always something. You were with him long enough, where did he have 'em stashed?"

"What? I don't know. We had some gold. I helped him dig some gold. He had a few opals too but I sold them. Small stuff. I sold that bit of gold. My aunty bought it off me, so I could have a bit of pocket money. I don't know anything about sapphires."

"Where did you dig the gold? That mine of his, eh? Where is it?"

"Tennant Creek. Up there past Tennant Creek. I know where it is, but I don't know what road. I can show you, I don't care. If you want gold just dig it yourself."

Obi paused for a moment, thinking, still trying to gather his wits, then added, "Maybe he's got sapphires. There's a shack up there, with a workshop, and a tool shed. He was pretty tidy. There might be a safe up there, I don't know. He made me stay in the shack when I knocked off. He just made breakfast and cooked dinner and wouldn't let me wander around. We had lunch down in the hole. I haven't got a clue, honest."

"All right then. Get up, have something to eat. You thirsty?"

Frank went stepped over to the side of the truck and leaning over pulled a big tucker box across. He lifted the lid and took out bread and butter, with some jam and a billy to make tea. He then lit a small gas stove and boiled a billy, and when he was done invited Obi to eat. Obi poured himself a drink of water first, from the side tank, rinsing his mouth and spitting it out before taking a deep draught. Lenny was at the back cleaning his face with a damp cloth but soon joined them and made a cup of tea before standing away to drink it by himself.

Twenty minutes later they were back on the road. Mile after mile went by, while Frank gave Lenny a long lecture on tact and diplomacy, and how you get things done by using your brain, not acting stupid, like a cheap thug. Lenny sat in silence, gazing out the window as the landscape slipped passed, and Obi just sank back into himself.

~*~

Back in Adelaide Sam and Peter were just starting out, after having been on the phone to Warmunya Community for over an hour, deciding at last their best option was to get a good sleep and start out early the next morning. At the community itself Bertram was out directing vehicles, refueling and filling the water tanks, making sure everything was in order, and by nine o'clock a small convoy was heading out along the track toward Puntayeri.

Frank and Lenny drove straight through, stopping occasionally for a piss and something to eat, with each taking turn as driver while the other napped. They didn't talk to one another all the rest of the way. Obi sat quietly in the middle, thankful. He let his mind wander, thinking through the options and finally deciding to let Peter take the lead. He'd be good. He'd think up something real smart. He'd know where they were headed, eventually, sooner or later, and he'd be waiting. Without allowing even a flicker of a smile to betray his thoughts, he napped on and off, dreaming about what he'd do when they got there. That Frank was cunning, like a fox, they'd have to watch him, but Lenny was thick as two planks. That would come in handy. We could use that sort of talent. He was pissed off already. Maybe that Frank wasn't so clever after all, cutting his force in two like that, leaving one half leaderless. Clueless.

Mile after mile slipped by. It took better than fifteen hours to reach Tennant Creek and it was dark as they drove though. Only the police paddy wagon was out doing its rounds of the fringe camps but they ignored it and drove on. At the service station just outside town they stopped to refuel, and just in case top up the water and check the vehicle over carefully. It was a good truck, apart from the ghost it carried; George had been a bloody good mechanic and seasoned bushman. These blokes had got a good deal trading their old truck in on this one, as soon as Sam had disposed of it, and before the mechanic had a chance to go over it and assess its true worth. Before he could see how well it was set up for desert travel.

Obi kept his thoughts to himself, feigning slumber. When Frank nudged him to wake up and go take a leak he yawned and stretched, rubbing his eyes, then clambered groggily out the passenger side and went off to find the toilet. When he finished he went inside to buy a six pack of cold Coke and an ice cream before climbing back into the truck to settle and wait for the others. He didn't have to wait long before they were off again, but he ignored them and finishing a can of Coke curled up and went back to sleep.

Chapter Fifteen

The mine site was tucked away. It was well off the main road, accessed by a small track leading down into a long gorge; almost a goat track but wide enough for the Landcruiser at a pinch. The entrance was hidden from the casual eye by a low stand of desert acacias, but the truck knew this place well, it had carted everything in.

Down in the gorge tall palms and eucalypts dominated. Even from the air one would have to have flown in at a particular angle to make out the buildings down there among the trees, set back in against the vertical wall. It was pretty as a picture. As they made their way gingerly down the narrow track off the wide flat plain above, Obi studied the place with new eyes, glancing cannily from Frank to Lenny and back again. They were both intent on negotiating the steep descent and failed to notice the gleam in his eye as he put final plans into place. Well, they weren't final, depending on Peter, but close enough. It didn't matter. He sank back into his seat and enjoyed the bumpy ride.

There was a small landing at the bottom, only big enough to park the truck with a bit of loading space either side, and room to turn around. Anyone would have thought George was a city bloke building on a quarter acre block in the suburbs, the tiny amount of land he took, even a bit of grass passing for lawn. Maybe he was, originally. Just in front was a shack, and alongside that a workshop with a tool shed added on behind it. They were well built, but the rest of the place was undisturbed.

It was a paradise in miniature, away out here in the desert. The colours were not such a deep glowing red; more ochres and yellows with patches fading to grey, and the greens more olive than citrus except at the tips, and for the tall palms catching the sunlight overhead, waving their fronds in the soft breeze. There was deep water here too, unfathomed, out of nowhere. It hardly ever rained this far out, only once in a blue moon, the gorge cutting into the top of the great aquifer extending across half the continent.

The moment the truck stopped and they were out, he headed off down the path toward the pool.

"Where the fuck yer think you're goin'?" Frank growled.

"Just for a swim, all right. I need a bath, I'm dirty, and I stink."

Frank turned to Lenny, thoughtfully, then back to Obi. "Keep an eye on 'im, will ya," he said out the side of his mouth. "I'll go scout around a bit." He then turned and strode up to the shack and went inside.

Obi watched Lenny for a moment, then he too turned and walked off, down the narrow path through the trees until he came to a narrow beach of sandy debris that had accumulated over the millennia, there at the edge of the water. He promptly stripped and hung his clothes up off the ground, draped neatly over a small tree. Lenny had come down the path and was watching him, so keeping him in the corner of his eye Obi half turned and took a piss against the tree trunk. Then he stepped back and waded slowly into the cold water, up to his chest, until he pushed off the sandy bottom with his feet and swam to the other side. Fat Lenny sat on a log, watching him.

"What are you looking at, fat man?" Obi called across to him. "What are you, a poofter or something? Bloody pervert."

"Just shut up, will ya."

"You're a bloody paedo. Like boys, do you?"

"I'll fuckin' clock you, little shit you are."

"Frank!" Obi yelled suddenly, "Frank! Frank!" at the top of his voice. "Frank, come here! Help! Help! Lenny's trying to hurt me! He's trying to get me! Help!"

Frank came running down the path to see Lenny get up off the log and Obi out there in the water screaming.

"Told ya to fuckin' leave 'im be, ya fat cunt. What are ya, a fuckin' poofta."

"What? I didn't fuckin' touch 'im. You told me to keep an eye on 'im, 'n that's what I was doin'. Nothing' else."

But Obi drowned him out. "Don't let him near me. Tell him to go away. I won't get out 'til he goes away. I don't want him looking at me like that."

Frank turned on Lenny. "Just get the fuck up to the truck, eh. Can't even fuckin' trust ya to keep an eye on a stupid fuckin' kid. You're bloody useless, shit, gotta do every fuckin' thing meself."

Lenny backed off, shaking his head, then turned and walked slowly back up the path.

Frank turned angrily to Obi, there in the water. "Just get out, will ya! Out of the fuckin' water, now."

Obi swam back across and made his way timidly up the bank, covering himself with both hands.

"Turn around, Frank. Stop looking at me," he complained. "I don't want you looking at me while I get dressed."

"Ah, God all fuckin' mighty. I never heard so much bullshit. Get yer gear on, yer fuckin' little cunt, or by Christ I'll fuckin' lay the boot in meself."

He promptly did as he was told. He sat on the log to put on his shoes and socks, and the moment he was done Frank grabbed him by the arm and shoved him bodily up the path.

"Show me this fuckin' mine, all right. You said there was a hole in the ground. Where the fuck is it?"

He turned slightly, raising his right arm to point down along the edge of the pool. Saying nothing, back at the truck he led the way around the workshop and past the tool shed onto another path following the contour along under the wall of the gorge. They walked on a way, as they went Obi explaining to Frank how the thousands of years of washing away the gorge, way back when it rained a lot more, had created this accumulated gold deposit, this rich seam that George had found. Nobody else knew about it, but with nobody else to talk to George had raved on and on at him explaining how the geology of the place had struck lucky.

They soon came to a rough gantry, with steps cut into the soft rock leading down and down into a more or less horizontal shaft following the seam along a damp long-buried erosion deposit with the gold in it. But there was nothing there apart from the mine working itself. George being neat and tidy kept all his gear up in the shed, and once Frank realised there was nothing to be gained here he took Obi by the collar and they went back up the way they had come.

Lenny was sitting in the truck with the door open to catch the light breeze, but Frank ignored him shoving Obi aside into the workshop. There was a small lathe in there, and a welder and generator set mounted on a set of skids with the exhaust vented through the wall, with a variety of power and hand tools arranged neatly on modular shelving. There were lengths of steel on racks along the back wall, and a range of off-cuts stacked alongside; nothing out of place and nothing out of the ordinary. Frank stood there a while gazing around, then grabbed Obi again by the shirt and took him outside and over to the shack.

There was nothing out of place there either. The small fridge had been switched off and the door left open. There was no food going mouldy, and nothing stale or unkempt. Frank went through the cupboards but there was only a stash of tinned food and a carton of beer that had been broken into with a couple of bottles missing. The empties were there on the sink with a clean glass, washed and drained. The bed was made. The place was clean and tidy, nothing.

Bending down Frank picked up the carton of beer and stepping outside put it in the back of the truck, calling Obi to stay with him he wasn't finished here yet. Around the back in the tool shed, however, there were only picks and shovels, brooms, rakes, hammers, prospecting pans, a set of electronic scales on a work bench, and a box full of loose ore bags, all empty.

Back at the truck Frank leaned against the front mudguard, scratching his head. Lenny sat quietly, saying nothing, while Obi reached into the cabin for a can of Coke and opening it sat on the grass and started to drink. Frank leaned forward and knocked it out of his hand. He picked it up and wiped away the sand, but instead of taking another drink looked up seeking reassurance.

"You're the only one who knows where they are. You're the only one with him. Why don't ya just fuckin' tell us and we can all go home?"

"I don't bloody know," Obi protested. "I never saw any sapphires. I never heard anything about sapphires until you blokes came along. Why don't you ask those fellas at Warmunya? They buried him. I was out cold. I didn't know what was going on. First thing I know we're out at Puntayeri, when I woke up, and he was already buried. Under a sheoak. Out there by himself. Sam maybe knows, but he was with me, looking after me. Those other fellas had the truck, Bertrum and Eduard, all those fellas."

Frank stepped away from the truck, and for a moment Obi thought he was going to hit him again, but instead he paced around deep in thought, then arriving finally at a decision said, "All right, get in the fuckin' truck. We'll go find out, eh?"

Chapter Sixteen

In Tennant Creek, at the police station, the sergeant was sitting there at his desk wondering what on earth George Summers' truck was doing traveling north back through town. He only noticed it casually out on patrol, but at the same time it shouldn't have been there. He'd put it on the train to Adelaide only a week or two ago. When he rang, the South Australian vehicle registry advised him that it had been traded in at a used car yard by Samuel Francis Flanagan, and repurchased the very same day by one Francis Harold Lacy of Emerald, Queensland. At that moment, by sheer coincidence, a request came through on the radio to check the driver's license of said Sam Flanagan, who had just been pulled up on the main street with a rear tail light and left indicator not working. He had a native boy with him, Peter Wilson Napantjarra from Warmunya, supposed to have been at school in Adelaide. What were they doing back up this way so soon? The sergeant said bring them in, we'll have a little chat.

Ten minutes or so later Sam and Peter were ushered in from the front desk, and he sat them down.

"Cup of tea, Dr Flanagan?"

"No, thank you. We are rather anxious to be on our way. Is there anything we can help you with?"

"Just curious. I thought it was you coming through town last night, in George Summers' old truck."

Sam showed no sign of surprise, or interest. "No, we sold it, traded it in. It's not quite what you'd call a city car. It wasn't set up very well for my use. Maybe someone else bought it and came back up here with it."

"That someone wouldn't be Frank Lacy, by chance? Know 'im?"

"Heard of him. The Warmunya people know who he is. I know from them. Knocks around the gem fields and comes across here occasionally."

"Is that so? Excuse me a moment, will you."

The sergeant went out and spoke to his receptionist, then picked up the phone and made a quick call before returning.

"Big mob cleared out yesterday, from Warmunya. Do you know anything about that?"

Sam shrugged. "Tribal business, probably. They don't talk to me much about that side of things, unless I happen to be there. Even then they keep quiet if there is something up." He paused. "Sergeant, are we being kept for some reason? I mean, a tail light and blinker is no crime, I can fix that on the way out. I need to refuel anyway."

"No. No problem. You're free to go."

"Thank you." Sam stood and went out, Peter shadowing him.

"Ah, Dr. Flanagan, How's the Lennox boy? Get him back home all right?"

Sam stopped, gazing at the big policeman a moment, then nodded curtly. "Yes, he's fine, no worries."

The other simply nodded back, then watched closely through the glass door as the two got into the Landcruiser and drove off.

"All right, get me Ned Miller again," he said out loud. "Call Warmunya and tell him I want to know what the hell is going on up there. Then fuel up and be ready to leave. We might go for a little drive, I think, make it a day or two, chop chop."

~*~

Out on the track past the Warmunya turnoff Frank noticed the tire marks stretching ahead of them. There were three or four Landcruisers at least, so he stopped and got out to stride back and forth examining them. He paused, scratching his whiskers thoughtfully, then stood staring intently through the glass windshield at Obi. He came back to the driver's window.

"What's goin' on? Yer want ta tell me about it, or what?"

"What? I don't know. There was a big corroboree up here, maybe they're still cleaning up. Might still be some people at Puntayeri, you'll be able to ask them, won't you. They'll be able to tell you something about your sapphires. Maybe."

"Just get in, Frank," Lenny interrupted. "Fuck ya. We'll find out soon enough."

Frank glared across at the fat man before slowly turning his gaze back along the track, eyes narrowed and nose twitching like a dog sniffing out trouble.

"The track's chopped up a bit." Obi said suddenly. "When we get there I'll show you, else you'll get bogged. It's about twenty kilometres. That's where George got bitten by the snake. The women got bogged there too, and you'll have to go around. They might have marked the track by now, but anyway I'll show you when we get there."

That was enough. Frank sighed and shook his head, then got back in and started off again. He kept quiet all the way, glancing occasionally down at the boy sitting there innocently with his third can of Coke, and once or twice sneeringly across at Lenny. Just past the sandy patch Obi insisted on stopping again so he could pee, then casually left the empty Coke can there at the side of the track. Frank made him go pick it up, telling him not to be so untidy.

Two hours later, Sam stopped there as well, while Peter got out and checked the footprints before returning to the truck and nodding, said Obi was there not too far ahead now.

Half an hour after that two police wagons made their way quietly past.

The great breakaway could be seen sticking up out of the desert for many miles, but as they came into the dune country proper they began to lose sight of it again. It reappeared over each new sand ridge before they lost it tobogganing down the loose sand on the other side, only to climb steadily in low gear up the next slope until finally the enormous red outcrop filled the windscreen. Coming closer there were no vehicles apparent, although the young trees and heavy undergrowth down there among the gardens could have hidden a whole fleet if need be. Driving slowly past the lone she-oak Obi pointed out George's grave there underneath, but almost immediately on skirting the edge of the garden they were stopped by a line of painted warriors blocking the track, spears ready. They sat in the truck, frozen, waiting.

"Um, better get out I think, might be diplomatic." Obi suggested, trying to hide a smirk.

The two men stepped gingerly down from the truck. The moment he was clear Obi ducked away to join Bertram and the others. One of the older boys took his arm and led him to the side while some of the men closed ranks around the two visitors and shoving them along took them away up onto the escarpment. Bertram sat down under the shade and motioned Obi to come sit with him. The other boys gathered around.

Bertram looked him up and down, nodding slowly to himself.

"That gran'father finish up. He like you, that ol' fella. You good boy, comin' up now, comin' all that way. Big sorry time now. Big dancing comin' up. Proper funeral time, eh?"

Obi gazed sadly off into the distance, but sat saying nothing for a while. He turned and said softly, "Peter is coming. Right behind us I think, not too far. Sam is coming too, I bet."

Bertram nodded. "We wait here little bit, eh? Little bit longer."

One of the boys went up to the tank and brought fresh water and some food. Obi sat and ate, then took a deep draught and leaned back waiting. Soon one of the men came down and after a quick word with Bertram got into the truck and drove it back along the track to park it next to the she-oak, not beside George's grave there but right on the top of it. He left the keys in the ignition and stepping down out of the cab walked back, right past where they were all sitting, and without a word went up the slope to join the others.

A little over two hours later they heard another vehicle coming, and within about twenty minutes Peter and Obi were reunited. They went off with the other boys while Bertram had a brief parley with Sam. Instead of coming up to the big cavern with the rest they took a stroll around the garden, talking quietly, but before they had got too far more vehicles were heard arriving and they went out to meet them. Two police wagons stopped there on the track and the sergeant got out wanting to shake hands.

"We seem to be running into each other lately, sergeant. It there anything we can do for you?" Sam wanted to know.

"Just out for a wee drive, Dr Flanagan. Thought we'd call in on the way past."

"Six hundred kilometre round trip, sergeant. That's a wee drive? You'd think something was up, wouldn't you?"

"You think so?" the sergeant replied. "Like to tell me about it?"

"What? Nothing to tell. Somebody died, and people are arriving for his funeral."

He leaned forward slightly and taking a notebook from his shirt pocket scribbled, *Vincent Wilson Napantjarra died three days ago. He is being buried here.*

"Sorry, sergeant," he continued, "but I cannot say his name out loud. That name cannot be used any more, it's finished. This place is a sorry place right now, properly. Big funeral going on. We'd ask you to respect that."

The sergeant nodded, then turned to indicate the truck standing out there by itself, under the she-oak. "Find out who was driving the vehicle?"

"Yes, as you mentioned, Frank Lacy and a couple of mates. They are here for the funeral, apparently. I doubt they'd enjoy being disturbed."

"Here for the funeral? Can't be disturbed, eh?" The big sergeant nodded, then tipped his hat. "Right you are then, we'll be off."

Stepping up to the lead wagon he shrugged, and audibly sighed. He turned to Sam, tipping his hat again, then wearily got into the vehicle and turning around drove off. The other wagon followed suit.

Chapter Seventeen

They had Vincent trussed up in blankets and old canvas, high up on a stick platform in a tree growing out of the rock way up there on top of the breakaway. Old men and women were sitting around on the bare rock, keening and wailing, there where the gnarled roots struggled and wormed their way into the cracks and crevasses seeking a toehold. Fresh blood dripped and ran from gashes on their scalps, where they'd been beating and punishing themselves in their sorrow, down their backs and shoulders forming tiny rivulets across the stone surface.

The place was older than Adam. A person could see forever from up there. Obi nodded to himself, then turned his back to the old tree and gazing out across the plain to the far horizon started crying out loud. Peter joined him, and as he did so the old women set their wailing to a new pitch. They all took their turn, singing and crying until sundown when in the dying rays they made slow progress back down to ground level.

Some of the men still painted in their colours were there with torches. As those coming down from the top joined them, they made their way through the gardens then up a sharp incline over the low saddle in the ridge-top, down the back following a narrow path through the undergrowth, until they came to a cleft in the rock face and filed through. There was a small amphitheatre in there, big enough to hold forty or fifty men without anybody from outside noticing. The walls were covered in elaborate paintings like the main cavern on the other side of the ridge, but with no roof the sky was open to the sun and the stars. Frank and Lenny were standing there in the middle, with a group of men close around them. As the last of them filed through the crack Bertram made Sam stand to one side and watch while he took Obi and Peter by the hand, and led them into the middle to stand before the two white men.

At his signal one of the men came forward and undid Frank's trousers, then Lenny's, so they both stood in shirts and underwear with their pants down around their ankles. Bertram then began an angry tirade in his own language. Halfway through he stopped and reaching over took a spear from one of the men. It had a long iron-wood point, clean and sharp with no barbs, and as he paced back and forth yelling and abusing the two he began stroking the tip of it up and down Frank's bare thigh. Taking the spear back occasionally he turned aside pointing at Obi, then at Peter, and went back to ranting and stroking Frank's leg with it.

Abruptly his anger rose to a fever pitch and before Sam could do anything to stop him he drove the point right through Frank's outer thigh, past his femur and out the other side. Frank stood there in shock, his face taut with the pain, but he didn't move. Sam started forward but he was held back, while the two boys simply stood speechless. Lenny wet himself, then pale as a ghost slowly toppled sideways in a dead faint. Bertram tormented the spear tip, running it through and back again, all the while watching Frank's face. When he didn't move he relaxed. He nodded finally then slowly withdrew the point and handed the bloodied spear back to one of the men.

Indicating two of them and raising his arm he pointed east to the Queensland border. There was no mistaking his message, and at that he turned abruptly on his heel, tapping both boys on the shoulder, and strode purposefully out. The two followed close behind, Obi white as a sheet and Peter trembling with dread, leaving Sam there sweating and shaking. Recovering sufficiently he stepped over to Frank who was beginning to crumble, and helped him to the ground. He stripped off his shirt and tearing it into strips quickly bandaged the damaged leg, staunching the flow of blood. Ignoring Lenny he stood and berating two of the others made them pick Frank up off the ground and carry him out.

Down past the garden they set him down again. Bertram had taken George's rifle and was over there at the she-oak shooting out the tires of the truck. He held both boys back, talking quietly to them, instructing them, not angrily but patiently, brooking no more nonsense from either of them. The truck settled onto its rims. Bertram stepped over and opened the cocks of the fuel tanks, and looking inside the cabin took the bucket still there and filling it with petrol began liberally dousing the truck. Satisfied finally, he walked back up to one of the camp fires and taking a burning stick stood back and threw it into the truck. It went up with an almighty whumph! The she-oak caught fire as well, but after watching it a moment to make sure it was well alight Bertram turned on his heel and bade the boys follow him back up into the cavern.

Sam went across to his own truck, and taking his first aid kit came back to start treating Frank. Pulling his leg out straight he set it in a long splint to stretch the thigh muscle and stop it from cramping up, then swabbing with antiseptic neatly stitched the ragged bleeding gashes in his thigh front and back. He worked silently, sullenly, turning aside from Lenny as he staggered past ashen and disoriented, simply waving to one of the men to take him away. The sutures finished he wrapped a clean gauze bandage right around the wounded thigh, then reaching into his kit took a syringe and gave Frank a tetanus injection from the portable fridge in the truck, before finally knocking him out with a dose of morphine. He helped load him into the back of one of the Landcruisers belonging to the community, and as they started off spoke quickly to the driver.

"Take him to Camooweal Hospital, all right. Just don't go anywhere near Warmunya or Tennant Creek, or that sergeant will be onto you. Maybe go out along the back road behind Warmunya."

The other said nothing, simply nodded, and drove straight out past the burning truck there on top of poor George's grave.

The night passed. Sam slept fitfully, his swag rolled out on the ground next to his vehicle, and at first light he got up and went over to the tank for his swim and a bath. The pump was quiet. Small families of colourful finches flew in formation with him, less than a metre from his fingertips as if seeking his intimacy and comfort. He turned, gazing about, then back again to the bare acacia branches where their rainbow breast feathers lit up as the sun broached the horizon, turning the muted pastel shades of the dawn into a fairyland.

Presently the two boys came down and joined him in the tank. When he had bathed and cleaned himself up Obi waded across to speak to him.

"Sam, when we get home we'd better check the claim on George's gold mine," he said, his face serious, "see if it's registered. I don't think he ever pegged it, you know."

Sam looked him in the eye, nodding gravely. "Yes, we'd better do that. That's important, isn't it."

THE END

ABOUT THE AUTHOR

As an anthropologist, novelist and writer Gil Hardwick is a gifted and imaginative author. Over many years working as a field ethnographer in the vast Australian inland he has met real characters and had real-life adventures, bringing his personalities and his plots to vibrant life. Writing from life, he neither shies away from real social issues and at times confronting dilemmas.

Well worth reading.

www.ingramcontent.com/pod-product-compliance
Lightning Source LLC
Chambersburg PA
CBHW071407170626
46811CB00003B/1292